LISCHE

Wynn Johnson

LISCHE

Vanguard Press

A CIP catalogue record for this title is
available from the British Library.

ISBN 978 1 784652 98 2

*Vanguard Press is an imprint of
Pegasus Elliot MacKenzie Publishers Ltd.*
www.pegasuspublishers.com

First Published in 2017

**Vanguard Press
Sheraton House Castle Park
Cambridge England**

Printed & Bound in Great Britain

Introduction

He laid claim to fifty-three thousand acres of untamed Kentucky wilderness. The land was free for the taking, but it was wild and mysterious. The year was 1857 when he returned to North Carolina and married his childhood sweetheart. They returned to Kentucky in the spring of 1858 and built a small but beautiful farm. In 1860, they had a son. They named him Cossberg. Life couldn't have been sweeter, until the spring of 1861, when the Civil War began.

Two out of the four years of the war Lische hid in a cave to avoid fighting. History has never made it clear as to whether he was a coward, a scoundrel or a conscientious objector. Either way he would pay his dues and fight his own battles. He fought snakes, wild animals and the elements, just to stay alive. His name was Elisha, but folks who knew him called him Lische.

His son, Cossberg, would one day amass a fortune from his land, and then sell out cheap to a coal company. His grandson continued to grow that fortune in the form of land investments, fine horses and banking. His great grandson became a war hero serving with the Marines in World War Two and Korea.

Lische walked the Earth for more than a hundred years; he died in 1944. His grandson and father of the war hero was born in 1885, and died in 1989, at the age of one hundred and three. He was my great-uncle, my friend and my mentor.

Lische is a book that reads like a novel, but the people and events were very real.

Chapter One

The young man placed the final stones in the northwest entrance to his grotto creating a barricade. Closing the entrance would serve two purposes. One was to conceal the light from his campfire and the other was to keep out the cold wind that would soon blow nonstop in the months ahead.

The refuge he created for himself was nothing more than a space under large rocks. It was one of nature's mysteries. It was as if some strong and powerful force had stacked countless boulders, leaving just enough space with a curved entrance for human existence and concealment. To enter, Lische had to be on his hands and knees. Once inside, he could almost stand erect. The room was about eight feet wide and ten feet long. There was a small opening in the back, where smoke from his fire could escape.

It wasn't easy living like a mole under boulders of rock when his young wife and son were snug and cozy just three thousand feet down the mountain. Although there were better caves in the mountains for a man to shelter in, they were just too far away to serve his purpose. He was close enough from this location to look after things. If he should happen to hear rifle shots, it would only be a quick dash down the mountain. For better or worse, this was what he had chosen, and it was too late to change his position. He didn't consider himself a coward; he just didn't want to fight anyone. Besides, how could he leave Sally and three-year-old Cossberg to fend for themselves in this Kentucky wilderness?

It was mid-September 1863. His name was Elisha, but most people just called him Lische.

Lische had seen a poster tacked on the wall in the mill at Wheelwright. The poster had a list of names, and his was one of them. The poster was a subtle reminder of every man's duty to help protect the state's rights and the obligation to report for military service. Even though the state of Kentucky had remained neutral during the war, both the Union and the Confederate Armies were inducting young men.

People told stories of men dying by the thousands. But to Lische, it wasn't patriotic; it was ludicrous. What was all this nonsense about state's rights, anyway? How could state's rights possibly have any bearing on his life out here in the wilderness?

The ranking officers commanding these boys to fight were heroes of the war with Mexico. The fuel that kept it all burning was the hate between President

Lincoln and Jefferson Davis. Lische just couldn't find enough reasons for sacrificing thousands of lives and ripping apart a young nation. Lische felt those old warmongering veterans of the Mexican War should go out into a field, settle their differences and leave everyone else alone. He kept telling himself he was not a criminal, yet he was ever conscious that he could face a firing squad from the Union Army as well as the Confederates. He could be executed not for something he did, but for something he failed to do.

Lische climbed to the top of his grotto and sat down on his backside, resting his arms on his knees. He was completely exhausted. He had also never felt so alone, even though he was a frontiersman who had spent countless hours in the wilderness. A nagging question kept burrowing deeper into his mind, demanding to know if he was doing the right thing, or just being a coward. Either way, this was how it would be, at least for now.

A cool breeze quieter than a whisper gently rocked the treetops high above him, causing a single yellow hickory leaf to drift slowly to the ground. Weeds and small trees close to the ground had now lost most of their leaves, as if they were shrinking to seal the forest floor. This too was a reminder that the hot, lazy days of summer were coming to an end. Soon the autumn rains would lead to a long and cold winter.

Lische wondered if Sally felt the same sadness and insecurity. She was a strong and confident woman who had been through a great number of trials along the path to this new life in the wilderness. There had been but a few surprises. Before they settled in Kentucky, Lische had tried to paint a most true and honest picture for her, as rough and tough as he could. But Lische had also promised her a good and rich life, if they could find a way to tame the land he had already claimed.

As he sat at his grotto, his mind began to wonder back in time. The last six years had been a long, hard, and continuous journey. This was just one more exhausting obstacle to face. He had no clue how long it would last.

Chapter Two

Lische was born on the sixteenth day of August 1840. In the spring of 1857, he set out from New Bern, North Carolina, with his older brothers, Harvey and Daniel. There were thousands of acres of unclaimed and untamed wilderness in Kentucky, along the western edge of the Cumberland Plateau. This land was there for anyone strong enough to take it and make something of it.

Taking ownership of unclaimed land was a simple process known as a tomahawk claim. First you had to make sure the land wasn't already taken. You then had to place your unique mark on the trees or rocks along its border with an ax or tomahawk. The final and most important part of claiming land was to record it with the land office.

The brothers had gotten the idea after reading about a fellow up in Ohio by the name of Simon Kenton. Some decades before, he had laid claim to a large chunk of Ohio. (They had failed to read the part stating that Kenton had died a pauper.)

Daniel was eldest of the three. He was twenty-four, strong and commanding. Daniel made the rules along the way. Harvey was a quieter man. He was just as much of a frontiersman as his older brother, but he was obedient and willing to follow. Lische had grown up fast. At sixteen, he had already chosen Sally to be his wife. However, he knew he would have to earn her. And in North Carolina, he was penniless.

For almost a year, the brothers worked nonstop to claim a track of land four miles wide and just over fifteen miles long. They then headed to Frankfort to register their claim. They took with them a mule, which they traded for a six-foot crosscut saw, a splitting maul, some wedges, and other tools for shaping trees into cabins. They would build their cabins, and then return to North Carolina for the winter. Come springtime, they would make their way back to their new homes.

They returned to their claim and hastily built cabins for Daniel and Harvey near present-day Melvin, two miles east of Wheelwright. This was close to other settlements, which offered at least a few amenities, such as a gristmill and general store.

Lische, on the other hand, wanted no part of civilization. He wanted seclusion, peace, and quiet. So he got on his horse and rode east, following an animal trail along the south bank of what would become Left Beaver Creek. He and his brothers owned every inch of this land, but they had only surveyed and marked it along the ridgeline never venturing deep into the hollows. As Lische ventured in further, he saw the land was a wonder to behold.

It consisted of narrow hollows, steep mountainsides, and an abundance of creeks and streams. The most fascinating aspects were the natural resources. The ground was covered with no less than a foot of soft black dirt. The size of the trees was proof of just how rich the soil was. There was very little underbrush beneath the giant trees. As he rode slowly along, Lische glanced up from time to time to try to get a glimpse at the blue sky above, but very little sunlight reached the forest floor. He passed through groves of beech, maple, oak, hickory, and poplar. Chestnut trees towered straight and tall above them all. The deep shade was cool and damp, and the air was filled with the pervading smell of vegetation.

As he followed the narrow animal trail along the banks of the creek he found many twists and turns. The creek had many branches where smaller streams flowed in from other hollows, or canyons. The morning sun was ahead and slightly to the left, so Lische kept following the creek to the left.

About three miles east of Harvey's cabin, he came to another fork. There was no path along its banks now. Along both sides of the creek and as far as he could see up the mountainsides, waterweeds stood almost as tall as a man. Even though their stalks can be as thick as an inch, waterweeds are a tender plant, easy to thrash. Lische would go on foot from this point.

He cut a strong walking stick from a small hickory tree and began to hack and slash a path along the creek bank. It seemed to take hours, but he finally broke into a clearing. There was another fork in the creek as one branch took a sharp left turn and up a steep, rocky gully. From the looks of it, an ancient landslide had diverted the creek and plowed away everything in its path, leaving behind a flat, grassy plain.

I've found it, he said to himself. *This is where I will make my home.*

The sun was setting, and the songbirds were at their loudest. He followed the creek up the rocky gully, where he found a spring. The water ran cool and clear toward the main stream. Fresh water and no more than seventy-five yards from his cabin site.

He knew he should have made his way back to his brother's camp, but Lische just had to sit for a while. He formed a picture in his mind, a complete layout of his future farm. The house, the barn, a fenced area for the livestock and just above it all was another clearing for gardening.

He walked back down to the main creek. There he found a large rock on the bank and sat with his feet dangling just above the water. It was getting dark now. The birds had almost stopped singing. Those sounds were replaced by the sound of frogs and the cascade of water.

Lische wondered what his girl, Sally, would think of his plans. He wondered if she would even have him. After all, he was penniless. Well, he was penniless, but he was very, very land-rich. Then he wondered how he could convince a pretty young girl to live a primitive life here in this wilderness. But he wouldn't even let himself think of alternatives, for there could be no one but Sally.

He got up and walked to the edge of the forest. He stopped once again to look back at his new home, one that would be a place of peace, quiet, and repose. He hated to leave it. He walked back into the clearing for one last look before starting for Harvey's cabin. Yes, this was to be his new home.

Lische then turned to make his way back along the path he had hacked out earlier. He could still see a hint of green, but the forest grew darker by the minute. It was an awkward trek as he tripped and stumbled along.

He had been a woodsman his entire sixteen years of life, but there was something unnerving about this forest and these mountains. For one thing, he had never seen so many snakes. He was not afraid of them when he could see them and confront them face-to-face. But this was different. Now and then, he could see shadows of them slithering through the water or hear soft hisses as they made their escape through the leaves. It was getting darker by the minute.

This was unlike the forest of the East Coast. He was seeing and hearing things completely foreign to him. There were grunts, growls, barks, and squawks, even though most animals are afraid of man. He hadn't carried a gun on this trip. But then, he had planned to be back to his brother's cabin before dark.

He began to analyze the sounds, separate them, single them out, and try to identify them. Just about every animal was capable of emitting more than one sound. A bear, for instance, could make all manner of sounds. It was the same with a deer, a raccoon, or a mountain lion.

This was a strange land, one that hadn't been inhabited by humans for centuries upon centuries. Kentucky was sacred ground to the Native Americans. The very word itself translates to 'Land of Plenty'. It was set aside for hunting only and closely guarded by the Cherokee to the south and the powerful nation of the Shawnee to the north.

However, he just couldn't shake the feeling of being watched. There was no doubt about it—something in the darkness didn't want him there. Again, he wished he had carried a gun. But what good would it have done? He could only have fired shots into utter darkness.

Something flew past him from time to time. He couldn't see it, but he felt a gentle swoosh, then a section of the trees would sway high above him. At first, he tried to ignore it. But then it would fly past him again, each time getting closer, as if to assure him he wasn't imagining things.

He couldn't wait to get back to his horse. He tried to focus on the path, but again—*swoosh*. It seemed to come down from the very top of the forest, fly past him, then return to the tops of the trees.

Lische finally made it back to his horse, only to find him too nervous and jumpy to ride. He kept looking all around as he groped at the knot in the reins. When the knot was finally free, he held the reins about a foot from the horse's nose and started back along the three mile trek toward his brother's cabin.

It felt like hours, but he finally arrived to find Harvey sitting on the front steps smoking a homemade pipe.

"It's about time, Lische. I was just about to come looking for you," Harvey scolded. "Is there something wrong with your horse? Why aren't you ridin' him?"

There was a pause before Lische responded. "I'm not sure what's wrong with him. He was just too jumpy to ride."

Daniel came out of the cabin and leaned against the porch post. "Maybe you spooked him."

"What do you mean, *I* spooked him?" Lische asked.

"Well, you know, a horse can read you through and through," Daniel said. "If you're afraid of something, then he'll be afraid as well, without even knowing what scares ya."

Lische thought for a moment, and then replied, "I suppose that's possible. It's just that I've never seen a forest as dark as this one. And the sounds, have you heard those haunting sounds?"

Neither Harvey nor Daniel spoke for a time. Then Daniel said, "Well, I'm sure they're animals here that are new to us. But we'll just have to deal with 'em."

Lische then spoke softly, almost as if he didn't want his brothers to hear him. "What if it's not animals?"

Lische watched closely for his brothers' response. He could tell his brothers had heard strange sounds as well.

Finally, Daniel spoke. "You know, Lische, we're men of God. We were raised to believe in spirits both good and evil. If there are evil spirits watching over this land, we'll have to deal with 'em."

"And how do you suggest we do that?" Lische asked.

"The worst thing you can do is show fear," Harvey said. "If you show the slightest sign of fear, the spirits will run you outta here. You have to stand tall and straight and let 'em know you're not goin' anywhere. There's a lot at stake here. We have a chance to have somethin'—somethin' far more than we could ever have in North Carolina."

Daniel sighed. "I think we should turn in—get some rest. Tomorrow we'll start building a place for your future family."

With that, the three of them bedded down at Harvey's place for the night. They didn't have glass windows. Shutters would have to do for now. Lische had always felt completely safe sleeping under the stars, but even there in the cabin, he still couldn't stop thinking that he was being watched. He lay there on his bedroll, staring through the open shutter, watching the treetops swaying in the summer breeze, and wondering if he had imagined the whole thing.

The sun was only touching the tops of the mountains when they had finished a breakfast of bacon and biscuits, gathered their tools, and were off. The grass was heavy with dew when they walked into the clearing at Lische's home site.

There was no need for planning. All three knew exactly what had to be done. They only stopped long enough for Harvey and Daniel to envision for themselves what Lische had described. The two men never spoke but nodded in approval.

Harvey then walked to the edge of the clearing and selected a tall, straight beech tree. There were softer woods available; however, beech would last through the ages. In just a couple of minutes, Harvey had cut a notch in the direction he wanted the tree to fall. Daniel then joined him with the crosscut saw. Soon the first of many trees hit the ground. Lische trimmed away the branches, cut the log to the proper length, hitched two horses to the log, and pulled it to the cabin site. When he returned, Daniel and Harvey had another log ready. This continued until almost sundown.

The next day, the logs were put into place. The third day, the roof logs and the wood shake shingles were installed. Door and window shutters would be installed when they returned from the coast in the spring.

There was very little conversation, but it was an unspoken fact that they were happy in their work. It was a warm day, though nowhere close to as hot as it could have been in late June. There was a pleasant smell in the air, that of crushed weeds and sawdust drying in the summer sun. With their cabins now functional, they would rest for a couple of days before starting their long trek to North Carolina.

Chapter Three

On the third day of July 1857, the brothers got underway, arriving in New Bern the first week of August. Almost immediately, they began to sell possessions they could do without or that might be cumbersome on their trip. Therefore, they sold almost everything they had. They did, however, purchase three additional horses, one work mule, and two spring wagons.

Even though they were ready, they would winter in North Carolina and wait until the first week in March to start the long journey across the Blue Ridge Range and farther into the Appalachian Mountains. The mountain ranges of the eastern United States are somewhat conjoined, sectioned or divided only by river valleys. They planned to use the cash they had accrued to buy passage on the train wherever there were tracks along the way.

That fall, Lische asked Sally to accompany him on several long evening walks. They held hands or walked arm in arm for hours. Lische spoke excitedly about

Kentucky. He spoke of the sights and scenery he had seen along the way. He told her about the abundant wild fruits and berries that grew along the edge of the clearing. He talked about deep forests, blue skies, freshwater springs, and clear running steams.

He talked about the cabin—how it was small now, but that he had plans to enlarge it. He described in detail just how his farm was going to be. But he just couldn't bring himself to ask the right question.

One day as he was describing his bright and shining future, Sally stopped him abruptly. "So, Lische, are you planning to build all this by yourself?"

"No," he said. "I won't build it at all unless you share it with me."

They returned to her home and asked for her parents' blessing to be married. Her parents were sad that their Sally would be going away, but they knew there was no stopping their headstrong daughter. Lische and Sally were married on the thirteenth day of February 1858.

Lische and Sally headed out in March, along with Daniel, Harvey, and their wives. The trip took weeks. Creeks, rivers, bluffs, and the towering Blue Ridge mountains had stood in their way. Following ancient Indian trails and paths of the few settlers who had gone before them, they made their way north and west. The Wilderness Road would have been ideal for their travel, but settlers had abandoned the road around 1840. By

1858, there was little left. The almost tropical forest quickly reclaimed any man-made path or clearing left unattended for even a few short years.

They arrived in Kentucky the first week of April 1858. Each couple took their respective cabin, and work began immediately. The first order of business was to plant a garden. With abundant wildlife, meat would be easy to find all year round. But for fruits and vegetables, they would have to make maximum use of the growing season.

That first year was nonstop hard labor. After planting the gardens, they installed door and window shutters in Lische's cabin and built a large stone fireplace that covered the entire south end of the small cabin. They built a small barn for the livestock and placed brush along the perimeter of the clearing for a makeshift fence. They planned to be there a long time, but for now, much of what they did was temporary with plans to enlarge or replace it later.

The unearthly spirit—or guardian, as Lische called it—continued to appear now and then. He never mentioned it to Sally, for he was sure she would be frightened. And he wasn't sure how he could explain it. At any rate, the spirit had done no harm so far. His theory was that the spirit, or spirits, were here to watch over this land. And so far, they did not disapprove of what they were seeing.

The spirit didn't appear every day, but it always appeared when he least expected it. It didn't frighten him anymore. He never mentioned it again to his brothers, but he wondered if they had ever seen it. Perhaps it was meant for him only.

He even wondered if it was real. And just when he was able to convince himself it wasn't, it would appear. On a day when there was little or no breeze and the trees were motionless, he would catch it out of the corner of his eye. He would sit and watch for hours on end without seeing anything, and then it would arrive. An entire treetop would bend, or a large branch would dip as if a heavy weight had been slowly placed on it.

One lonely afternoon, he decided to try communicating with the guardian. He called out to it and had one-way conversations with it. However, it didn't appear to respond. He never stopped talking to it, he just accepted it as his companion—his alone.

That first winter wasn't nearly as warm and cozy as Lische and Sally had imagined, but they knew exactly how to make it so for the next winter. They planned to have more of everything when winter came again. By the first week of April 1859, they had already planted potatoes in a large section of the garden. They would have a root cellar and a full pantry. They would make the cabin warmer and have much more firewood. Lische spent an entire week clearing a trail to the mouth of the hollow, where he had tethered his horse during his first visit. From there, Harvey and Daniel had already cleared the rest of the way. Now they could take the spring wagon all the way to Wheelwright.

Lische and Sally were as happy as a couple could be, and everything was going just as he had promised. They didn't get tired—they were too excited to be tired. They worked their gardens, built fences, and added on to or improved almost everything from the year before.

Then in September 1859, Sally told Lische her time of the month had passed her again. There was no doubt about it—she was pregnant. On May 13, 1860, they had a son. They named him Cossburg.

Their land lay at the headwaters of what would later be called Right and Left Beaver Creeks. Twenty-two miles northwest, the creeks joined, and just downstream from there, they flowed into the Big Sandy River. Their claim was about as deep and hidden along creeks and mountainsides as one could imagine. Perhaps this was why so much of it had been unclaimed before the brothers arrived. This didn't matter to Lische and Sally, however. They loved peace, quiet, and seclusion.

Everything had gone according to plan or perhaps a little better. The garden had produced abundantly that year, even though rain had been sparse toward the end of the growing season. The new ground Lische had cleared had produced very well. And as soon as the weather turned cooler, probably late November, he would butcher a hog. Pork could be preserved by smoking or packing it in salt. They had made every possible preparation for a fat and cozy winter.

Life had been good — until now. Lische had warned Sally of every worst case scenario he could possibly imagine, but the war between the states had taken them completely by surprise.

As Lische hid out in his grotto, Sally had never complained, even though she had left everything that was civilized back in New Bern. When their wives became homesick for the ocean Harvey and Daniel quit their claims and returned to North Carolina. Sally had no family at all in Kentucky now except for Lische and little Cossburg. Yet she went about her daily chores seemingly happy.

There alone in his cave, Lische couldn't help but believe he was betraying Sally and little Cossburg. But serving would surely have been worse. He was sure he would have never seen his family again. What would have happened to his family without him? And how would Sally have ever been able to return to North Carolina?

Still, he kept thinking he had made a terrible mistake. One way or another, the life and the dreams for which they had traveled so far and worked so hard were probably gone—or certain to be altered.

The only thing Lische had to look forward to was sneaking down to see his wife when the signal was given. The signal was a lantern. If all was clear, Sally would climb about one hundred yards up the mountain in front of their cabin and swing the lantern back and forth just after dusk. From his vantage point atop his grotto, Lische could see the signal.

But there would be no signal for a few days. Settlers had been steadily pouring into the area, and villages were beginning to form. Young men from almost every family were called to military service. A lot of people were asking about Lische and his whereabouts.

Lische had to lay low and wait until everyone thought he was away with the army, or until he was virtually forgotten.

Chapter Four

As the days passed, Lische survived on squirrel, rabbit, and woodchuck. He lost a considerable amount of weight, but it wasn't from the poor diet. Rather, it was from the constant worry and agonizing loneliness. Every night, he sat on the cliff above his cave and watched for the signal from far below. He had lost track of the days, but he knew it must have been mid-October, for the leaves were in their peak color and steadily falling.

At last, he saw a faint glow from far below. Excitedly, he grabbed his long tom rifle and rushed down the mountain. He stopped about two hundred yards from the house and listened for any unusual sounds. He then crept cautiously toward the house.

Sally met him at the door. After a long embrace, she said, "Lische, I'm worried sick. Cossburg became sick with a fever. I had to take him to see a doctor."

Lische held her firmly at arm's length. "What's wrong with Coss? Where is he?"

"He's fine," she said wearily. "He's sleeping. The doctor said it was nothing to be worried about. But the people, Lische," she said, wringing her hands. "They're asking all kinds of questions about you. Their sons and husbands have been taken, and they want to know if you have gone to fight as well. Oh, Lische, how long can we go on like this?"

Lische turned toward the door only to see their beagle, Rascal, with his nose to the crack in the door. He growled, his hair standing on end. Then there was the sound of hoofs on the rocky path. Lische slipped through the backdoor and hid in the chimney corner.

The rider called out, "Hello in the house!"

"Yes, sir, what is it that you want?" Sally answered as she stepped out onto the front porch.

The stranger, a somewhat older man cleared his throat. "Well, my missis said she saw you at the doctor's office today; that your little boy was sick. She sent me to check on you."

Sally replied, "Yes, he had a temperature, but he's all right now."

"I see!" said the stranger.

At first, Lische had felt very uneasy for not grabbing his gun on the way out. But now it seemed the visitor had good intentions.

"Where's your husband, ma'am?" the stranger asked.

"He's away, mister," Sally said. "He won't be back for a long time."

"Well, that's the reason we thought we should look in on you. We're only a few miles away if you need us. There are lots of young ladies who are fending for themselves with this dang war and all. I was too old to have to go, but that could change. They said it would be over in just a few months, and here we are in the third year of it."

Sally nodded, she was eager for him to be on his way. The visitor had assumed Lische was away fighting in the war, and Sally didn't want him to think otherwise.

"We really mean it," the man said. "If you need anything at all, just let us know. If you need food, firewood, or whatever, we live just above the trail, a quarter of a mile this side of Wheelwright."

As the man rode away, Lische felt even more guilt. Sally was right—how long could they live this way? He thought about poor Sally and the fact that she had to hitch up the team and take their son all the way to Wheelwright to see the doctor. And this was a close call with the visitor almost seeing him. He spent that night in his own bed, but there was little rest. He and Sally were both restless, worried that if he came home too often like this it could mean disaster.

Just before dawn the next morning, Lische made his way back to his hideout. He had to find a way to occupy himself, or he would go insane. He knew he would need a large supply of firewood for winter, so he would work on that. He would gather and cut wood into lengths about three feet long. However, a large cache of firewood neatly stacked just outside his cave would be a dead giveaway. So he would cut and store it in small bundles in various places within a hundred yards or so of his hideout. This project would take some time to complete.

As he spent his days working on the firewood, he thought about the many things they needed to get done around the cabin as well. They had been in the process of canning fruits and vegetables when this whole thing started, but now Sally had to finish it alone.

The cabin's winter supply of firewood was another matter. His plan was to cut and stage it in small stacks during the day, then hitch the team to a sled, haul it in at night, and store it under the lean to behind the barn. Sleds were the vehicle of choice in the mountains. Using a wagon on steep grade could be dangerous to your horses.

All this would have to wait, though. He wouldn't dare take a chance on coming down the mountain until he was sure it was safe. After Sally's trip to the doctor, too many people were asking around and possibly dropping in on her. They had both agreed he should lay low for a while.

In the beginning, Lische and Sally had Harvey, Daniel and their wives for companionship, but it's different now. Harvey and Daniel had given up, quit their claims, and returned to North Carolina in the spring of 1862, and now it all belonged to him, for what it was worth. He knew Sally had been lonely for the companionship of neighbors. That's probably the reason he had sold off some small parcels to new settlers (that and to help pay his property taxes). Had he not sold those parcels, though, there would not have been anyone around to ask questions about his whereabouts.

When evening came, Lische climbed atop the grotto, although he knew there would be no signal. He took a long look toward the mountain along the horizon to the northwest. He owned that mountain and everything in between. In fact, if he were standing on top of that mountain looking at the mountains farther to the northwest, he owned those as well.

Lische's grotto was just below the top of a tall plateau known as Collier Rock, so named by the early explorers who surveyed the region some decades before. Lische had chosen this location along the southeastern border of his domain, because it was least likely to be searched. Just a hundred yards from his hideout to the top of this monolith was unquestionably the most spectacular scenery in the entire Appalachian range.

Lische spent countless hours gazing at the mountains of West Virginia and the Blue Ridge Mountains of Virginia to the east. But then there were the majestic Cumberland Mountains to the southeast and in the direction of his former home in North Carolina. He could never become complacent to such a splendor. How could it be that nature had created these lovely mountains, carefully carpeted them with a perfect forest older than the ages, and then filled it with so many fascinating creatures?

He would watch as small cotton clouds seemed to come out of hiding, only to be consumed mid-flight by the summer sun. Early morning fog would form in the valley floors. By mid-morning, it would thicken and rise bright and white to conceal all but the tallest peaks. It looked as if he could step from his perch and walk on the surface of the fog to the waiting mountaintops. By early afternoon, the fog would dissipate entirely, and the lush green valleys would magically reappear.

Wealth was measured in terms of property in those days, so Lische was a very wealthy man. However, Lische was alone again with lots of time to think about the mess he had made for himself and his family. He began to ask himself questions: Was it all worth it? Was this land even worth anything? Even though it was densely forested with virgin timber, that timber would be very difficult to harvest. There were no roads and not enough water in the streams to float logs. There was ample flat land to grow enough vegetables for home use, but for the most part, it was too steep for commercial farming.

Whether good or bad, the land was beautiful to look at, it belonged to him, and no one could encroach upon it without his permission.

Chapter Five

It was now late November. Seeing the lantern had become routine. The mountain stood just a little under three thousand feet in height, yet it was a long hike to the bottom and back. One had to use or create a zigzagging path, which made the journey even longer. It would have been quite treacherous to descend the mountain in a straight line, as the mountains are steep, and there were many cliffs and gullies. To climb the mountain in a straight line would have been rigorous and next to impossible.

This is not to say that Lische couldn't have done it. He was toned and conditioned from head to toe. At twenty-three, he was in his prime. In height, he was average for the day—about five feet six inches. His hair was blond, and his eyes were blue. They were a well-matched couple, he and Sally. She was a buxom lady with light brown hair and hazel eyes. Just like her husband, Sally was always prepared for life's surprises on the frontier. Little Cossburg's features were equally derived from his parents. He was a slender child with blue eyes and hair so blond it was almost white.

Lische knew of his good fortune. He had it all, if he could only hold on to it.

Lische spent his days hunting or gathering firewood. He had only been in hiding for three months, and already he had burned all the dead wood that was close by. Each day, he had to venture a little further to find firewood. Wild game was also becoming harder to find. In the dark, overcast days of late autumn, almost all birds and animals were naturally camouflaged. To add to this, it was the time of year when heavy fog and drizzle shrouded the mountaintops.

Just before Christmas 1863 Lische made a trip down the mountain. Things looked completely normal. There was still plenty of firewood, and the food shelves were still stocked with plenty. Lische would always check these things. He would also check the perimeter around the cabin, looking for evidence of unwanted visitors. He wanted to know if he or his cabin were being watched, for there was so much at stake. His search was very thorough. He looked not only for footprints but, leaves that were pressed flat to the ground, or a broken tree branch that hadn't been broken before.

Now back at his grotto, he placed a wool blanket over the rock wall to keep the wind from blowing through the cracks. He kindled a small fire and opened the supplies Sally had packed for him. The package was like all the others except for a news dispatch.

How odd, he thought as he unfolded the article and began to read.

It was a story about a great battle that had taken place that summer at a place called Gettysburg, Pennsylvania. The battle had begun July 1, and it lasted three days. There were fifty-three thousand casualties. The president had made a speech there in November to commemorate the battle.

Lische's first thought was, *Oh, the tragedy.*

During his visits home, he had read about other great battles as well. Ten thousand bodies lay dead along a wagon trail at a place called Antietam. More recently, twenty-two thousand had died at Chickamauga. Wouldn't this be enough to bring any government or governments to their senses? Lische was sure he would have been one of those casualties had he served. It was sometimes weeks or even months between times when Sally would venture to Wheelwright and bring back a newspaper. He wanted to be informed, but dreadful news of the war was deeply depressing.

Slowly, a puzzling thought came over him. Why did Sally place this article in his supplies? Was it to keep him informed, or was there a deeper meaning? Was Sally telling him in her own subtle way that he was a goldbrick, neglecting his duties? Was she trying to make him feel guilty for not serving? Or was she reinforcing the notion that he would have been killed if he had gone. Well, it did make him feel guilty, whether she meant it that way or not.

Lische kept remembering all the promises he had made to Sally. He still believed he could keep them— but not if he went off to fight in the war. What would happen to Sally and little Cossburg if he failed to return? Perhaps she could find a way back to North Carolina. Perhaps she would fall victim to robbers or wild mountain men.

There was no time for second guessing now. Good or bad, his destiny was sealed.

One morning, he could hear a faint but familiar sound coming from a hollow to the southwest. Lische listened closely. Yes, there was no doubt about it. It was the sound of an ax. He focused his attention in the direction of the sound, and then he saw a treefall creating a small opening in the forest. No mistake about it—he was going to have a neighbor. This was not at all an unwelcome sight, for that particular land was not his, and his cabin was more than five miles from this newcomer.

Who knows? Lische thought to himself. Perhaps one day when life was somewhat normal again, the families could be friends. Sally would love that. Even though she was accustomed to life in the wilderness, he was sure she would welcome a visit from a neighbor. To sit and chat with another woman, to share stories and experiences is human nature. He was sure Sally longed to talk about things only another woman could understand. Sally never complained, but he knew she longed for these things.

Each day, Lische walked to the edge of the cliff to watch the progress. The sound of the ax continued, and the opening in the forest grew larger. Finally, Lische could see the new neighbor hard at work carving logs for a cabin.

Lische remembered days not so long ago when he and his brothers had built their cabins. It was a skill born into the frontiersmen of that era. They cut away knots and curves in each log with every blow of the ax. They carved one side of each log completely flat and formed for the inside walls. They heated a metal rod to burn holes in the logs, and then they drove in wooden dowels to hold the logs in place. With his team of horses, they pulled the heavy logs into place. Small branches were saved for making furniture, and everything else was cut into sections and stacked for firewood. The most rigorous labor in building a home was gathering and placing the stones for the fireplace. Using a tool called a Froe; they split shingles from red oak logs. The doors and window shutters were made of heavy half log and hinged with thick leather. The final task was the chinking. They took smooth gray clay from the creek bottom and mixed it with straw, then forced it by hand into the cracks between the logs.

Yep, Lische said to himself. *That poor fella's got a lotta hard work ahead of him.*

One afternoon when boredom was taking its toll on Lische, he decided to venture down for a closer look at his new neighbor. He didn't want anyone to notice him and he didn't want to answer any questions; he just wanted a closer look. As he got closer he could hear the pounding of hand tools. He stopped about a hundred yards from the site and parted the bushes for a better look. He just couldn't believe his eyes. What appeared to a woman in a light green dress and bonnet was swinging a heavy wooden mallet splitting shingles from a red oak log about twenty-eight inches long and a foot wide.

Lische watched for a few minutes and he wondered what this woman looked like, but her back was turned. On the other hand when a woman swings a mallet like this one it's probably more than he wanted to know. Lische just winked his eye, with a quick twist of his head and a click of his tongue he said to himself, *A man sees some crazy things out here.* With that, he started back up the mountain.

Chapter Six

Lonely days came and went with fog so thick in November and December that he had to creep down to within a hundred yards of the cabin to watch for Sally's signal. Lische spent his days gathering wood for his campfire or hunting wild game. Food was becoming harder to find. The shelves at home were replete with canned vegetables, and there was plenty of pork hanging from the smokehouse rafters, but Lische couldn't risk too many trips home. Also, with three months of winter still to come, he didn't want to take food from his family.

Lische eventually succumbed to hunger, loneliness, and bone-chilling cold. He spent most of January snug in his warm cabin with his family, carefully concealing himself whenever visitors appeared. Hiding for Lische was always half-hearted. He was constantly questioning himself as to whether or not he was doing the right thing. If he were to be discovered by a neighbor, the hiding would be over. If he made the decision to come out of hiding he would surrender to the authorities. He would not give himself over to a band of roving ruffians.

Then one day Sally returned from church at Wheelwright with rumors of a roundup. Officials were looking for dodgers of military service. Lische had no choice but to return to his grotto in early February. His life seemed to be even colder and lonelier than ever.

Lische needed meat in order to survive, but it was too risky to return to his cabin. He knew it would be days or even weeks before the coast would be clear. So one morning he set out two hours before dawn, moving over familiar paths until he reached an area new to him where the hunting would be good. Deep snow increased the labor of every step. Everything he did seem to be harder, for his heart was sick with the disappointments of life.

At last it was dawn. A red sun's light flowed across the snowy mountaintops. He had expected to have seen a deer or something by now. It's strange—when a person feels down and depressed, all of nature seems to work its magic against then.

Throughout the day, Lische trudged onward through the snow. Late in the afternoon, he saw two deer standing on a ridge just about a half mile to the north. They were completely out of range. He would have to move closer. By the time he got to the ridge, the deer had gone down the other side of the mountain. Lische found their tracks and followed until he finally sighted them. However, as he moved, the deer also moved.

At last, just before sunset, he was close enough to try a shot. It was a downhill shot of only about a hundred yards. He took a few minutes to catch his breath and calm himself before laying his rifle across a log to steady his aim. Whether he would have food or whether he would go back hungry to a cold cave depended on this moment.

Lische held his breath and squeezed the trigger. There was only a click. He just couldn't believe it. What a time for a misfire. Perhaps the cap was bad or the powder was wet. Whatever the case, he would have to reload and try again before dark quickly descended. Fortunately, the deer had not seen him.

This time, the gun cracked. The young doe fell dead.

Lische rushed to the fallen animal and quickly field-dressed the deer to lighten the load for the trip back to his hideout. He started back on the long journey, retracing his tracks through the snow. As he reached the first mountaintop, the sun was already gone. Turning to the east, he could see the encroaching night. It would be fairly easy going if he stayed on the ridgeline.

His feet tingled, and he feared frostbite, but the rest of him was warm from the labor of carrying the heavy deer up the mountain. His trek back to his cave would be faster than his trek out. On the way out, he had needed to move slowly, with silent stealth, following the deer. He could move much faster now. Still, he realized that even a quick pace would get him back to his camp only by midnight.

All hint of daylight was gone, but he needed a short break. A large tree trunk lay across the path ahead, so he decided to sit and rest for a minute or two. Ridgelines in these mountains do not run in straight or level lines, but upward to peaks and back down again. Lische had stopped just below the crest of a peak. Was he two-thirds of the way back or only half, he wondered?

It was a crystal clear winter night, the stars were bright, and a half-moon made the night amazingly bright. It felt so good to relax, and he wasn't sure if he could regain the strength to continue. But he also knew that if he were to fall asleep, he would probably freeze to death.

The deer felt much heavier when he picked it up. As he swung it over his shoulder, something drew his eyes back down the path. *What is that?* He asked himself. He was sure he had seen something, but what?

Lische suddenly came to the realization that he was being followed.

He rushed onward, forgetting all about his fatigue. He turned frequently to look. Sure enough, they were still on his trail and slowly, cautiously closing the distance. *Must be coyotes*, he thought to himself. If it were wolves, they would have already been upon him.

Finally, Lische could see Collier Rock about a half mile away—and just beyond it was the safety of his hideout. As he turned one last time, he knew the predators would surely overtake him before he could reach it. He decided to try and kill one of them and perhaps that would scare the rest of them away.

Lische took careful aim at the lead animal and squeezed the trigger. Again, only a click.

In his excitement after killing the deer, he had forgotten to reload. How utterly stupid he felt. That was a mistake one simply could not afford to make here on the frontier.

He yelled and barked as loudly as he could to frighten and confuse the animals, hoping it would buy enough time to reload. Nervously, he poured the black powder into the muzzle, his fingers numb from the cold. He dropped at least two caps as he finally got one into place.

Lische took aim again. The gun roared. He wasn't sure whether the rifle ball had hit the animal, but the predators disappeared.

Lische couldn't have been happier when at last he reached his hideout. He dropped the deer near the entrance, stood his rifle against the rock wall, and dropped onto his bedroll, but only for a few minutes. He had a few chores to complete. After that, he could relax. He would not allow himself to doze that night, though. He would have to stand guard. If those animals were as hungry as he was they would surely come for the deer again.

He lit the lantern and got the fire going. He kept his back against the rear of the cave, and he waited. Even though the animals never came, Lische spent a long and restless night with a watchful eye on the entrance.

As he sat there, staring, the head of a large black animal suddenly appeared. It appeared to be a large dog. Its face was contorted into a snarl showing large white teeth, but there was no sound.

Lische leaned to the right, groping in the dim firelight for his rifle. He had to take his eyes from the beast for a split second to locate his weapon, which he was sure he had placed beside him. To his terror, he realized the rifle was out of reach, standing in the far corner of the cave.

That split second was all the time the animal needed. It didn't rush or pounce; it walked the few steps slowly, never blinking or growling. Without taking its demonic gaze from Lische's eyes, it lowered its head, opened its jaws, and bit into Lische's right ankle.

Lische screamed, rolled to the left, and then straightened his legs as he awoke. It was only a nightmare. The pain in his leg was nothing but loss of circulation—he had fallen asleep cross-legged with his rifle across his lap.

It was well after daylight when he emerged from the cave to inspect the area. He found no tracks in the snow. He was comforted by that fact. He then skewered some venison on a stick and roasted it over the fire. After breakfast, he collapsed on his bedroll and slept until early evening.

Chapter Seven

The weeks dragged on into the spring of 1864. Lische had visited his home, preparing and planting the garden. He moved like a ghost through the garden on moonlit nights, pulling weeds and straightening plants. Fresh vegetables were finally coming into season by the end of May. Now he could slow down and just let the rich dark soil do the rest.

Lische strolled out to the edge of the cliff to see how his new neighbor was progressing with the cabin. He pulled out the telescopic field glass from the inside pocket of his coat. Peering down into the valley, he could see smoke rising from the chimney. *They must be cooking*, Lische thought to himself. *It's too warm for a fire otherwise.*

Once again his curiosity overtook him; he just had to see what his neighbor was doing. Again he crept down the mountain to where he could see what was happening at the new and small farm. There she was again, toiling in the garden with a hoe. She was chopping at the weeds with the vigor of a twenty-year-old man. This time she wore a red dress with a white bonnet, but she also wore large leather boots. Lische realized that a lot of women were forced to fill the role of their husbands while they were away with the army. Lische still wondered what the woman looked like, but again her back was turned. Beyond that he never thought much more about it and away he went.

Lische seldom saw it anymore, but he knew the guardian was looking over his shoulder. He wondered if the guardian was keeping watch over this settler as well.

Lische sat listening to the faint and peaceful sounds of his new neighbor's small farm below: the cluck of chickens, the snort of hogs, and the occasional whinny of a horse. It was late afternoon in the final days of May. It had been a hot, humid, and cloudless day. For the past month, the weather had been unseasonably dry. *Sure could use some rain,* Lische said to himself.

It was then that he noticed the sun sinking below a dark gray wall far above the horizon. *Now isn't that interesting?* He thought. *That could be the rain I just mentioned.*

He found a comfortable place and sat down to watch the approaching clouds. He saw a flicker of lightning and thought how spectacular it would be to watch a storm roll in from his vantage point on top of this mountain.

After about an hour, the cloud had hardly moved. *Ahh, maybe next time, this one's gonna miss us.*

He decided stroll back to his grotto and have something to eat before dark. After he had some cold meat and potatoes, he walked back to the edge of Collier Rock to see what had become of the cloud. Tall trees laced the sky above his hideout, but from the top of this cliff, he could see for miles in every direction.

He was surprised to see that the cloud was now covering nearly half the sky. It was almost overhead. The cloud was very unusual. There were no breaks in it whatsoever. It was smooth and dark.

Then there was another flash of lightning. He held his breath for the longest time before he heard a low rumble of thunder.

I guess it's not gonna miss us after all.

He sat down again and continued to watch the approaching storm. There was another flash of lightning and another rumble of thunder. This time, the lightning was a little brighter and the thunder a little louder.

Lische was somewhat mesmerized by the storm as he searched the horizon for the next flash or the next rumble. The flashes were more frequent now, and the storm appeared to be moving faster. Then a few large raindrops began to fall.

The storm took on dramatic changes during the next few minutes. Lightning stabbed at the mountaintops as if they were being thrown by Zeus himself. The mountains to the west faded into a wall of white rain. It was time for him to race for the safety of his cave.

Once inside, Lische removed the wool blanket from the stones at the entrance so he could see the lightning steadily flashing through the cracks. The storm was a constant roar as rain fell in torrents. It reminded him of something he had read in the book of Genesis about the great flood: *'The windows of the heavens were opened, and the springs of the earth burst forth.'*

Lische was completely snug, dry, and safe. He was comforted in knowing his family was safe in the strong cabin in a valley protected by mountains on all sides. He would relax and let the much needed rain fall.

Throughout the night, the storm would often awaken Lische. Lightning would strike, or the wind would drop a tree. At last he fell asleep just before dawn.

About mid-morning, a different sound awakened him. It was the sound of rushing water pouring from the mountains to the valley below—his home directly in its path.

Lische pulled on his boots and raced frantically down the mountainside. He was completely soaked just minutes after leaving the cave, the rain continued to pour and the trees and underbrush were dripping as well.

With no time for the zigzag path, he went headlong and straight down the mountain. Brush and thorns scraped at his face and arms. There were countless brooks and streams dumping into the main creek that flowed past the cabin. It was a shocking contrast to the trickle just twenty-four hours ago. As he got closer, he could see nothing short of a raging river just a few feet from the cabin.

He rushed through the backdoor to find Sally nervously pacing. "I'm scared, Lische!" she said. "I saw a large log float past. I think it has the creek dammed just downstream."

Lische rushed outside, running along the water's edge. His wife was right. Trees on each side of the creek had blocked the log from floating on downstream. Brush and other debris collected at the site of the dam. The water was rising fast and would soon surround his cabin.

Lische ran to the barn for the horses. They were jumpy and frightened of the storm, but he soon had them rigged together. Grabbing a set of plow lines, he led the team back to where the log was lodged. If the horses were strong enough to pull the log free on the far side of the creek, then he could release the log and let the water take it downstream.

There was no time to contemplate whether the plan would work. It happened to be the only plan he had for saving their home. He knew that every moment brought more debris to the dam.

He secured the plow lines to the log almost without thinking. Then it occurred to him that as soon as the log was released, the force of the water would surely pull the horses into the current. It would have to be split-second timing. As soon as the log was released, he'd have to cut the ropes instantly. The sharpest tool he had was a weed sickle hanging in the barn.

He ran back to the barn, only to realize that if the dam were to break spontaneously before his return, the horses would be lost. When he reappeared with the sickle, the horses were eager to get on with the task. He had hardly given the command before they were low to the ground and pulling with all their might.

Surprisingly, the log began to move almost immediately. It was dislodged, but then the plow lines tightened. Lische knew he better act fast. With an angled blow, he swung hard and fast, cutting the ropes and freeing the horses. The log and debris were whisked downriver. The water level began to recede immediately. He realized he had been careless in not removing brush and debris from the banks of the main creek. Perhaps he had been a little too cautious not to disturb the eggs or the breeding place of his treasured rainbow trout along the creek.

Lische returned the horses to the barn, and then entered the cabin. He peeled off his wet clothes and threw them outside. When the rain stopped, he would wash them in the creek and hang them out to dry. Sally was making food, for she and Coss had not eaten since the day before.

Lische sank into a chair, completely exhausted. It had only been about an hour and a half since he had awakened in the cave. But in that hour and a half, he had pushed himself to the limit of human endurance with not a moment to catch his breath.

After a lunch of hot pork, potatoes, green peas, and cornbread, they took little Coss and snuggled in bed for a long nap. The reposeful sound of the birds awakened them in the early evening. The flash flood had receded to a peaceful level, and there wasn't a cloud in the sky.

Lische ventured out to survey the damage. The house and barn were not damaged. The garden in front of the cabin had been completely washed away. Fortunately, they had other gardens on higher ground. Those had a little hale damage, but he was sure they would still grow and produce.

Sally stretched and yawned. "It's time for me to start supper."

"No, Sally—wait," Lische said to her. "We have to talk."

"Yes, Lische?" she said softly. "What is it?"

Lische searched for words. "Well," he said, "I've put you through a lot of hardship. Through it all, you've never complained. But twice now I've put you in jeopardy. The first time was just getting you here through the snakes and the wild animals and now this flood. Sally, I've decided not to hide anymore. I feel all these bad things are happening because I'm a criminal. It's just not fair for me to be safe here while men are dying in battle."

"Lische, that's not true," she replied. "And you're not a criminal. What if you hadn't been up there on that mountain today? Lische, we would have lost the cabin for sure. At least you were here to protect us." She gave a weary smile. "As far as hardship, life has been just the way you always told me it would be. Now we're beginning to prosper. We have land, we have our house, our horses and barn. We have food, and we are together as a family. All the things we dreamed of are here. Just look at this beautiful valley."

She reached out and took his hand.

"Lische, I love it here. We have to hang on."

Chapter Eight

The remainder of the summer passed uneventfully. One day, Lische sat on the edge of a cliff and watched a small herd of deer moving slowly along the ridge to the east. He had a hog back home ready for butchering. But he would take a deer now to last them until it was cold enough to preserve the pork.

It was the fall of 1864. He had been in hiding for more than a year now. *It seems like a lifetime*, he thought to himself as he walked back to the grotto for his gun. *It'll be a long and cold winter, but not as cold as it would be behind breastworks on a battlefield.*

It must have been about noon when he set out to overtake the herd of deer. November's dark and overcast weather had settled in, giving the distant mountains a shade from tan to dark blue and purple. Heavy fog settled rapidly over the mountaintops with a chill that made Lische shiver. However, the fog and dampness was very much to his advantage. Lack of visibility would enable him to move in close without being seen, and the wet leaves kept his footsteps almost silent.

He carefully crept over the crest of the mountain, and there they were. The herd hadn't moved more than a hundred yards from where he had first seen them. But suddenly the deer caught sight of him. They bolted, as swift and graceful as the wind disappearing down the mountainside.

They were all gone except for one large buck. He was perfect. He was strong and noble. His antlers were perfectly formed, his fur dark brown, his shoulders rippled with muscle. Instead of running away like the others, the old buck strolled out on a large rock, exposing a perfect silhouette against the sky.

It would have been a perfect shot, but Lische hesitated. He studied the old buck and his strange behavior. The deer just stood there, as if consigned to his fate.

The first thought to enter Lische's mind was, *How stupid could this old fella be? Doesn't he know I'm about to kill him?* Lische placed his right thumb on the hammer and cocked it back. He took a cap from his pouch and put it into place, never taking his eyes from his prey. Still the old buck never moved. He only stood waiting for his final breath.

Then Lische began to understand some things about the old patriarch. He carried the scars of many seasons of rutting. He had led his herd to safety many times, losing only those who could no longer keep up. He had sired many, while maintaining control and leadership. And now the old patriarch was willing to give in to nature and lay down the final sacrifice. He seemed to invite death and say to Lische, "My years have come and gone and now, you must take me first in order to get to my family."

Lische said to him, *Well, I'll gladly relieve you of your final breath.* He slowly placed the gun to his shoulder, taking careful aim. The gun was pointed dead center of the chest, a shot that would drop the deer painlessly. Lische's finger slightly trembled on the trigger as he held his breath. Then he lowered the gun.

"Oh, to hell with ya!" Lische yelled at the top of his voice. "Go about your way, ya crazy old fool! But if I ever see you again, I swear I'll... No, I probably wouldn't," Lische finally admitted.

The old buck gave a final glance as if to say, 'You had your chance.' He slowly walked away.

Lische took a sharp left turn and went along his way as well. He climbed mountains and descended into deep valleys. As hunger set in, he almost regretted not killing the old buck. But it was, as they say, 'Water under the bridge'.

He estimated he must have traveled more than twenty miles north east of his hideout. He followed the ridgeline and could see a river in the valley below. He could also see houses and farms along its banks. *That must be the Big Sandy. I must be near the village of Pikeville*, he thought.

Perhaps the wind had kept him from hearing the voices and the rustling of footsteps in the dry leaves. But now it was too late. The army patrol was no more than a hundred yards from him. As he instantly bolted, he heard someone shout, "There he is!"

Lische didn't stay to hear another word. He was running for his life. He heard a swoosh as a musket ball flew past him and crashed into a tree, then he heard the report of the rifle. The delay in the sound told him he was gaining distance on the pursuers. But the shot also told him he needed to be more careful. He began to dart from side to side and use as many trees as possible for cover.

Lische was exhausted and hungry, but he couldn't slow down. He ran in sprints of about a hundred yards, resting briefly behind trees or large rocks. At last, he paused long enough to catch his breath. He peeped carefully from behind a tree. Holding his breath, he listened and heard nothing but the wind. Emboldened, he stepped from behind the tree and looked through his field glass. He saw nothing, but taking no chances, he rushed onward.

Just then, a man jumped from behind a tree, directly in front of him, no more than fifty yards ahead. Lische was startled and confused at first. He wasn't with the patrol. This man appeared to be running for his life as well. As the man took off in the same direction Lische realized they were running for the same reason.

Few men could match Lische on foot in those mountains. He soon got close enough to call out to the man. "Hold up there, mister. We're probably on the same side."

The man slowed, then stumbled forward and stopped behind a tree. "Why are you chasing me?" the man asked. "You're not the army?"

Lische replied, "No. I'm running from the army as well."

The stranger was a gangly looking fellow, about the same age as Lische. He had a rather peculiar looking face, with a crooked nose and large ears. His hair was a dirty brown, and it hung to his shoulders. His green eyes didn't seem to focus. And he spoke fast and loud, almost as if he were afraid he wouldn't be given enough time to make his point.

They knew there was no time to talk. As they pushed onward together, Lische began to realize a few things. Lische had been blaming himself for getting too close to the Pikeville settlement and exposing himself to the army patrol. But now he realized they had been chasing this other fellow. He was the one who had ventured too close to the village. When they saw Lische, they simply mistook him for the man they had seen near Pikeville.

Too exhausted to go any further, they stumbled into a dry place under a cliff. They didn't dare make a fire, so they huddled together, shivering, until just before dawn. They then traveled southwest, back toward Lische's hideout, following the ridgeline that took a gradual turn to the west. Lische was back in familiar territory, but he didn't want to lead the army to his cave, so he stopped to look back. Again he took the scope from his inside coat pocket. There, following along their trail, was the patrol moving at a slow but steady pace. They had just passed a large and familiar boulder. Lische knew he and the stranger had passed that rock not much more than an hour ago.

For the first time, Lische contemplated the possibility of being caught. He began to wonder if he were reaching the limit of his endurance. He then imagined the worst consequences of giving up. Would he be shot on sight? Would he be taken back to stand trial; court-martialed and jailed, or would he be stood before a firing squad?

Lische was tired. Every bone and every muscle in his body ached. It was now mid-afternoon, and a thousand thoughts ran through his mind. He began to formulate a plan for surrendering to the army. He would let fate run its course. But he would not give himself up without seeing his wife and son for the last time. He would not surrender to the men at his heels. They had already demonstrated a willingness to shoot him. He had to find a way to elude the men, and then he would turn himself in.

He gestured to the stranger to hold up. "Listen," he said. "If we're gonna escape these men, this is what we have to do. We need a burst of speed for at least two more miles, and then we need to cover at least another half mile without leaving a trace. I know a small cave that's perfect. It's in the middle of a pine forest just below the crest of the mountain. A man can be within fifty feet and not see it. I found the cave by accident. It's almost as good as my own hideout."

The stranger didn't argue and off they went.

As Lische had alluded, the entrance was nearly impossible to spot. They had to do some searching to find it, even when they were close to it. At last, Lische hurried the stranger into the cave. He found a red oak branch that had blown down the previous summer. Its dead leaves were still attached. He pulled the branch over the entrance.

Lische then instructed the stranger to make himself as comfortable as possible. They were to remain completely silent and motionless until the danger had passed.

They sat for what felt like hours. The glow of the late autumn sun was turning red. Soon it would be dark. It had been two days now since either of them had eaten. They were just beginning to think they could breathe easier when they heard footsteps and voices. It was fortunate for them that a large group of men couldn't move through the mountains without making noise. They couldn't have been more than a hundred feet away.

The voices grew closer. They heard one of the men say, "Look around. He couldn't have vanished into thin air."

Another voice proclaimed, "Yeah, but there's a million places to hide. The son of a bitch is probably worthless, anyhow. All we need is another goldbrick."

The first voice then said, "Well then, let's keep going and look for a place to bed down for the night. We'll set out again in the morning. If we find him, we find him. If not, then to the devil with him."

Lische and the stranger listened as the voices and footsteps faded in the distance. At last they could let down their guard and get some much needed rest. Perhaps tomorrow they would find food.

The small cave was much cozier than the place they had spent the night before. The floor was covered with fine white sand and leaves. The temperature inside began to rise from their own body heat, and soon they were sleeping soundly.

When dawn came, they crawled out into a cold, damp morning. The sun was shining on the mountainside to the west, but it would not reach this slope until later in the day. As quietly as they could, they crept upward until they reached the top of the mountain, where the sun was already bright and warm.

Lische took out his field glass for a long look around. He could see smoke from a fire. He knew the men had stopped for the night and were now cooking their breakfast. It meant the chase was over. Lische let out a breath, relieved and happy.

They turned west and headed toward his hideout at Collier Rock. When they arrived, they quickly made a fire, but they didn't bother to heat up the cold pork and potatoes.

At last, their stomachs were full and they were warm and comfortable for the first time in two days. They could do no more—they just slept.

Lische awoke to the sound of the man stoking the fire. It was still dark, but Lische felt completely refreshed.

"I wonder what time it is," Lische said.

"Oh, about three, I'd guess," the man answered. "You feel like talking a spell?"

"Sure," Lische replied.

The man said, "Well, to begin with, my name is Massie Tackett. I got me a cabin and a few hundred acres not too far from here, with a wife and two little kids. I thought I could sneak into Pikeville for a few things we need, but that's when I ran in to the army."

"So are they Union or Confederate?" Lische asked.

"Who knows? Union, I think. They looked poor and ragged, it was hard to tell. Anyway, I didn't stick around to ask 'em. I'll tell ya one thing—if they hadn't been on the other side of that river, I would've been cetched. They weren't more than seventy-five yards away. Lucky for me, there was a grove of pine trees nearby. I ducked outta sight and just started running and didn't look back."

It was then Lische's turn. "My name is Elisha, but folks call me Lische," he said. "I was deer huntin' when I ran into 'em. I guess they thought I was you. But it don't matter. I'm as guilty as you are. I've been hiding here for almost a year and a half. My cabin is down that way at the bottom of this valley. I got a wife and son too." Lische then asked, "Is that your cabin near the headwaters of Long Fork Creek?"

"Yep, it is. How did you know?"

Lische said, "Because you can see it from the top of this cliff. I've watched ya build it."

Neither man spoke for some time. Then Massie said, "Ya know, I haven't been hiding anywhere. I've been right down yonder, buildin' my cabin. Between that and working my gardens, I'm nearly worn out."

Then Lische said, "Well I'll tell ya one thing, that woman of yours is the hardest working woman I ever saw. I gotta admit, I crept down close enough to see what was going on at your place. The first time I saw her splitting shingles from a red oak log and then I saw her working in the field; hoeing corn like a man."

Massie blushed with embarrassment and said, "My little woman don't split shingles or work in the garden. She just cooks, cleans and takes care of the children. That there woman you saw, was me. I put her clothes on so I wouldn't get cetched. No telling who's sneaking around these mountains. Lische began to laugh hysterically as Massie appeared to become offended and demanded. "What's so funny?" Lische just continued laughing. Massie then said, "You won't think it's so funny when you get cetched."

Lische could see that Massie's feelings were hurt and he began to show sympathy. Lische said, "I understand Massie, whatever it takes. They were both silent for a short time as Massie began to smirk. Lische asked, "What's on your mind now, Massie?"

Massie said, "Well I was thinkin'. What iffin' one of them heathen Johnny rebs were to sneak up behind me thinkin' I was a woman and he was gonna steal a kiss. He'd spin me round and see my beardy face and big ears and he'd run all the way back to Richmond." With that both men began to roll with laughter.

When the laughter faded Massie began to speak again. "We came here from Portsmouth, Virginia, last summer. I told my wife I didn't want to go to the army, and she agreed. I told her if they came for me, then I'd go, but I wasn't goin' to hide from 'em."

"So then why are you hiding now?" Lische asked.

"Cuz I think the bunch chasing us, would've shot us on sight."

Lische thought for a few moments, and then he said, "Well, that's why I'm thinking of turnin' myself in."

It was as if he had thrown a cup of cold water in Massie's face. He jumped directly in front of Lische and looked him straight in the eye.

"No! No! No!" Massie said, shaking his head. "That's the worst thing you could do. Listen, man—this war will soon be over, and you'll be able to return to your family. Every time I get news 'bout the war, the North has won another battle. I don't see how the South can keep hangin' on. And when it's over, nobody's gonna care about rootin' out two crazy mountain men. You saved my life when you found me the other day. Now I'm gonna save yours. Stay put. It'll all be over soon."

Massie then crawled over to the cave entrance.

"Where are you going?"

"Home. To my family." Massie replied. "And I think you oughta do the same."

Dawn was breaking. "Yeah, you're probably right," Lische said.

After that, the two men went their separate ways.

Chapter Nine

Lische spent well over a month with his wife and little Cossburg, who would be five years old in just over three months. The little boy was too young to understand but old enough to start asking questions. He didn't understand why his father couldn't stay all the time with them or from whom his father was hiding.

In mid-February, Sally came home from church and said that rumors were once again going around that the Union army was scouring the mountains for deserters.

"I'm just gonna give up," Lische said.

"No you don't, Lische," she began to scold. "We've gone through hell with this, and you're not giving up now. There are also rumors that the war will soon end. If you turn yourself in now, they'll hang ya for sure. You have to tough it out until the war is over, then they'll have no use for you. We've come too far for ya to quit now."

So Lische decided he wouldn't quit, but he would return to his hideout to be on the safe side. He went to the smokehouse, took some salt pork and venison, and headed back to his hideout.

Three days later, he sat on the edge of the cliff looking over the dark mountains to the east. The snow had come and gone for the past two months, and it had been overcast for some time now with a pale sun shining through now and then. But there was definitely something brewing in the clouds to the west. He sat there for the next two hours until he noticed small pellets of sleet melting on the sleeve of his overcoat.

In case the storm turned out to be a big one, he brought in some of the firewood he had stashed. Large snowflakes were falling when he placed the last armload in his cave. With the temperature so warm, he was surprised to see snow instead of rain.

Lische then set out on a hunt. It would be good to have extra meat in anticipation of the storm. He knew he would've had better luck if he had set out before the snow fell. Game animals are warm blooded creatures. When bad weather sets in they huddled together in whatever shelters they can find. He would be satisfied with a squirrel, a rabbit or whatever he could find. Going back to the cabin for food was not an option. With snow on the ground, he would leave a trail straight to his hideout.

He didn't want to get his heavy wool coat wet, so he left it at the cave. He was used to the weather, and he didn't plan on being gone long. He took his rifle, powder horn, and a handful of musket balls, and away he went.

He looked up to see the last glimpse of the sun and guessed it to be about noon. The snow was falling faster and faster. It began to cover the ground and stick to the timber. It truly would have been a beautiful sight to see under other circumstances.

Lische had gone almost to the bottom of the uninhabited valley to the east when he thought he heard a voice. He looked up to see a large treetop sway. *Must be the guardian*, he thought to himself. He went a little further, and this time he was sure he heard a voice muffled by the heavy snow.

"Run, Lische! We're about to get cetched!"

Massie Tackett was running mid-stream through the creek below. Lische stopped and waited for him.

"We gotta go—they're after me again," Massie said.

"They're after YOU, not me," Lische replied.

"Well, if ya hang around, you're gonna get cetched too."

With that, they both began to run as fast as they could along the side of the mountain and in the opposite direction of Lische's hideout. They stopped only to listen for any sounds of their pursuers. Through the snow, they could see nothing beyond a hundred yards. And when they couldn't run anymore, they walked. They were careful to travel in a straight line to avoid the possibility of crossing the path of the patrol.

They were headed almost due south, a path that would soon lead them to the tiny settlement of Whitesburg.

The storm continued. Just before dusk, the wind began to blow. Their undergarments were wet with sweat, and their outer clothing was wet from the snow. The storm pounded them from every direction. They knew they had to find or make a shelter quick, or they would surely freeze to death.

They made their way to a tall peak, where they could look in every direction for a cave or even a thick pine grove. There didn't seem to be a single place sheltered from the wind. They glanced back to find the blowing snow quickly erasing their footsteps. With all his experience in the wilderness, Lische knew this had to be the worst winter storm he'd ever seen.

It was almost dark when they headed straight down the steepest side of the mountain—falling, sliding, and tumbling as they went. It paid off. About one hundred yards from the summit was a cliff about ten feet high that protruded from the mountain like a large thumbnail. The wind was now blowing hard from the right, so they slid down the right-hand side of the cliff and ducked under it. The cliff was only about six feet wide. It would take some work to make it a proper shelter, but it would have to do.

They rested for a few short minutes, but then the cold set in. Lische soon began to shiver.

"Look, Massie," he said, "we need to pile this place full of firewood. Then we need to bring in enough branches to block the wind. We'll arrange them like a half tepee. Only when this is all done can we rest for the night. So you go that way, and I'll go this way. Remember, firewood first, then look for pine branches."

The blowing snow stung their faces. Lische could no longer feel his hands. But they soon had enough firewood, and Lische found a long, straight hickory log that would be perfect as the center support for their shelter. He shouldered it and headed for the camp.

Before setting it up in the shelter, Lische needed to clear the snow and ice covering the hickory log. He thought the quickest way to do this would be to drop it against another log or something, with the impact breaking the ice. As he neared the camp, he saw a large black tree stump. He leaned over the stump and let the log fall.

There was a soft thud, then a loud scream. The stump turned out to be Massie, squatted in his long overcoat.

"Now ya done it!" Massie yelled. "You damn near broke my nose, my arm, and both legs."

Startled and a little angry, Lische yelled back, "What on earth are you doing out here like this?"

"I was restin', Lische. I can't take anymore."

Lische grabbed Massie by the arm and pulled him up. "Get to work, you sorry thing, before we both freeze to death! This is the second time you've caused the army to chase me, and I'm sick of it. Now get!"

They were finally able to make a fire and rest for the night. Despite their best efforts, the shelter did little to keep out the wind, and the fire was just enough to keep them from freezing to death. They were too miserable to sleep, so they just sat in silence. The snow stopped falling about midnight, but there was no let up in the wind.

Just before daylight, Massie said, "Look—there's a star. That's a good sign. Maybe the sun will be warm today. Ya know, Lische, I don't think there's any sound colder than the wind blowing through pine trees. I don't even like hearing that sound on a summer day."

Lische didn't speak.

"What are we gonna do, Lische?"

"Well, I know what *I'm* going to do," Lische said. "I'm gonna go about a half mile in that direction, and then I'm gonna head north. I'll be back at my hideout in two days. At least two days, if I'm lucky. And if I'm luckier than that, I'll find something to eat along the way."

Massie asked, "You're not headin' home?"

"No. I won't lead the army to my cabin. I'm goin' to my cave. If they find me there, they can have me. I'll tell ya one more thing, Massie—I will never run from them again."

Chapter Ten

The winter dragged to an end. Finally, it was time to start the garden. It was spring 1865. The rains came and went once again, but nothing to compare with last year's flash flood.

News about the war didn't reach them overnight, but what they had heard in January was that the Confederate army had weakened and the North was sure to win.

Some said the war would have ended nearly two years earlier at Gettysburg if General McClellan had followed General Lee in his retreat back to the South. Most folks thought Lee had been willing to talk peace at that point. But there was a bitter hate between President Lincoln and the president of the Confederacy, Jefferson Davis. Some said that hate had been the only remaining fuel for the war.

But by the first week in June, there was a different mood in the air. Perhaps it was the new hope that the war would soon end. Lische watched the sun set over the dark green mountains to the west. He then walked slowly back to the hideout, which was still almost completely hidden from the outside world.

He kindled a fire for cooking, not for heat. The evening was warm and peaceful. He heated up some pork and potatoes. After he ate, he leaned back to relax and listen to the almost tropical sounds of the night. There were night birds, insects, and the occasional wild boar, bear, or deer. Raccoons and other nocturnal animals produced noises that could entertain the worried mind. The whippoorwill was, without a doubt, the most beautiful sound from the forest at night, its song heard for miles.

Shortly after dark, a drizzle of rain started to fall. The dripping from the trees created a relaxing mood. Soon Lische drifted off to sleep, leaving the lantern burning.

Lische didn't know how much time had passed when he suddenly awoke not because of a sound but because of an eerie silence. The rain still dripped from the trees, but that was all. The voices of the night were mute.

A paralyzing shiver covered his body. There was a presence—he could clearly sense it but couldn't see it. Something, a creature, was just on the other side of the wool blanket covering the entrance.

He held his breath and fixed his gaze on the entrance. His gun stood no more than eight feet away loaded and ready, but he knew that if he made any sudden move the creature would attack. Lische could hear it breathing and sniffing near the blanket. In a small opening between the blanket and the wall of the cave, Lische saw dust blow as the animal sniffed, then exhaled.

Out of fear and instinct, Lische began to scream. When he stopped, he heard the sound of a heavy animal running away.

It was then he realized he was being stalked by at least two hungry mountain lions. He knew the big cats hadn't gone far, and he also knew they'd be back. The cats had no interest in Lische himself as prey; they had merely smelled his food. But they would attack him, just the same, for that food.

There was nothing as persistent or unpredictable, as a hungry animal and nothing as swift and deadly as a large cat. They hunted in pairs, with the female most likely to go in for the kill; while the male waited nearby to make sure the prey didn't escape. In this case, Lische knew the female had been at the entrance, with the male on top of the hideout, ready to pounce.

Sure enough, they returned only about ten minutes later. But this time, Lische's musket lay across his lap. He slowly brought the gun to his shoulder and cocked the hammer, which made a slight click. When the animal heard the sound, she emitted a low growl. At that moment, Lische fired a shot right through the blanket. The cavern filled with white smoke. Again, he could hear the animals running away.

It was two to three hours when the cats returned. Lische fired a shot the moment he heard them. And then he grabbed his pistol and ran from the cave screaming at the top of his voice, firing in the direction the animals had gone.

Lische crawled back into the cave with a sense of victory. He didn't think the cats would return. They didn't. However, he still spent a long and restless night. The hours dragged slowly until dawn. At first light, he got busy constructing a strong and heavy shutter to fasten securely into the opening each night before going to bed.

Summer was passing quickly. The gardens were producing well, and there was a feeling of tranquility in the air. On a bright morning in mid-August, Lische set out to explore his land. He found it to be even more enchanting each time he explored it.

There were tall groves of poplar and hickory. He walked along clear running streams with beds of soft green moss lining the banks. He felt the soft black dirt under his feet and thought about the fine gardening it would make. The forest was rich with nuts, wild berries, herbs, and spices. *It's a Garden of Eden*, he thought to himself. There was even sulfur and saltpeter, the key components for making gunpowder.

He stopped, placed his hands on top of his walking stick, and pondered: *What could I possibly do with all this land? Maybe I could sell it to other settlers, if or when they come. Or maybe I could grow and sell vegetables. But what would I need money for? Maybe I could send Coss to one of those fancy schools back East.*

It was late in the afternoon, and he was several miles from his hideout. It was time to start back. He decided to take a shortcut straight up the side of the mountain. It would be a tough climb, but it would reduce his journey by at least a mile.

It was sometimes one step forward and two steps back as the soft dirt gave way under his feet. He was sweating profusely as he fought his way upward through wild grapevines, large ferns, and underbrush. The sun was just above the mountaintop, brightly glistening and blinding him.

He had paused to catch his breath when he felt a slight tug on his breeches, near the top of his right boot. He looked down to see a young copperhead had struck and was trying to free its fangs from the fabric.

Lische knew the worst thing he could do was panic, so he slowly moved his walking stick from his left hand to his right in order to strike a downward blow. He shaded his eyes from the sun to see the snake. That was when he realized there were many snakes. Some remained coiled while others were outstretched and moving slowly toward him.

His first instinct was to jump carefully back down the hill to escape the snakes. But his feet were entangled in the vines, so he ended up tumbling down, dragging the snake with him. When he stopped rolling, he ripped the snake free and flung it as far as he could. Lische didn't stop, though. Down the mountain he kept going. He only wanted to distance himself from the snakes. Before he knew it, he was almost back to where he had started.

He took a moment to catch his breath and drink from the brook. He took a long look up the mountain. He would take the longer but safer way this time.

Right then and there, Lische suddenly decided he would not go on living this way. No more hiding out here in the wilderness. He would go home to his family, come what may. For almost two years, he had endured hardship, facing death on more than one occasion. He would be no worse off on a battlefield.

So on that day in mid-August 1865, Lische set out for home. It was well after dark when he reached a hill overlooking the cabin. His heart sank—there were two horses tethered to the post in the yard. Sally and little Coss could be in trouble.

Lische rushed headlong down the hill, and then plowed into the backdoor, knocking it open. Lische was just as shocked to see the folks inside as they were to see him. For there were his two brothers, Harvey and Daniel. He just couldn't believe it—he hadn't seen them in years. The brothers embraced.

"Harvey! Daniel! What on earth brings ya here?" Lische exclaimed.

"Lookin' for you!" Daniel replied. "We're thinking of settling down here, if you could spare a small patch of land?"

"Land I've got no shortage of," Lische said. "We'll look it over, and you just tell me what ya want."

As they all sat down at the table, Lische asked sheepishly, "Is the North still winning the war?"

"The war?" Daniel said with a puzzled grin. "The war's over. The North won. They chased old General Lee to someplace in Virginia called Appomattox. Lee signed the Articles of Surrender at the Appomattox Court House."

"When did it end?" Lische asked.

"Middle of April," Harvey said.

"So what happened to that fella Jefferson Davis?"

"Who knows, who cares?" Daniel replied. "But those Southern boys all got amnesty. I think everyone just wants to get over it and move on."

Lische was all aglow with relief and happiness. "I'll bet President Lincoln's a happy fella."

"No." Harvey said with a sigh. "The president's dead. Some actor shot him at Ford's Theatre in Washington just five days after the war ended."

The next day, Lische strolled about his farm as a free man. Somehow everything looked different. He could never find the words to describe it, but the world around him had taken on a completely new look. Perhaps it was what comes with happiness and the lack of worry. He then realized he had another reason to celebrate. It was August sixteenth, his twenty-fifth birthday.

He walked to the creek, where he knelt on a flat rock. He washed his face in the cold, refreshing water. It felt wonderful. It was the beginning of what would become a morning ritual, to wash away the worries and the troubles of yesterday and to give him a new outlook on a brand new day.

This practice was also passed on to Coss, one he completed every morning. The ritual became as important as any business practice. Even in winter, when the creek was frozen, they would use a stick or a rock to break the ice. They wouldn't towel off the water. They'd let it dry naturally, and leaving their collar and chest wet was a refreshing reminder of a new beginning. The face washing was reminder that this was a new day and any animosity toward anyone from the day before was forgotten.

Chapter Eleven

The years pass quickly when you're comfortable and at peace. It was a time of great prosperity. Lische and his family had everything a family of that era could possibly need. There was very little money coming into their household, but there was very little need for it. Soil conditions produced the finest in fruits and vegetables, and their livestock thrived on fields of tall green grass.

It had been ten years since the war ended, but there wasn't a day when Lische didn't think about it and the great suffering it had caused. Families had been torn apart. Men had limbs torn from their bodies. Nearly a half million chairs would be forever empty at dinner tables.

Lische couldn't imagine that suffering, but he had his own brand of pain left over from the war. His suffering was survivor's guilt. The fact that he hadn't done his part would haunt him for the rest of his life.

It's a well-known fact that it's easier to start a rumor than to stop one. In Lische's case, all it took was one person to start the rumor about his hiding away during the war. He never knew who had made his secret known, but he became synonymous with the word *coward*. He received the nickname, Groundhog Lische, for his hiding underground and he would carry that title to his grave.

Lische just lived his life and watched his fortune grow. Lische would choose at least one day a week to roam the mountains. He loved the cool mountaintop breezes, the quiet and the solitude. His weekly morning strolls often took him back to the summit of Collier Rock. Despite the years of rumors and name-calling, Lische never bothered to tell anyone how he had suffered greatly in his cave nearby. But looking from that towering peak somehow erased all that. From Collier Rock, he could see countless miles in every direction.

The years continued on. Early on a Monday morning stroll in May 1880, Lische sat down in his favorite spot to watch the sunrise. It was a peaceful morning. Robins were singing all around in the trees below.

Then Lische could hear a faint but foreign sound behind him to the west. It was mechanical. Puzzled, he walked to the western edge of the cliff. The sound was coming from a low pass about three miles to the west. Along with the sound, blue smoke slowly rose above the forest. Whatever it was, it was beyond his border.

But his curiosity started him immediately in that direction.

In just over an hour, he was standing on a steep ridgeline looking down at a great industrial happening. There was a crew of no less than twenty men toiling in the low pass below. They had what appeared to be a large steam apparatus with large gears and pulleys. It didn't take Lische long to figure out what was going on. They were building a tram with a heavy cable to haul equipment up from one hollow and lower it into another.

Lische headed home immediately. He just couldn't wait to show this to Coss. This was the kind of industry the twenty-year-old had promised his skeptical father would one day come.

Coss had been an enterprising young man since he was old enough to toddle along behind his father. When he was a child, one question only led to another, he just couldn't learn fast enough. Lische would answer his questions patiently, but cautioned him to remember the answers—Lische would become annoyed if Coss repeated the same questions.

And now Cossburg had grown in his father's image. He had attended school and enjoyed learning. Academics were needed for the future he envisioned for himself, but other areas of education interested him even more. He knew his father's estate would one day fall into his hands, and he wanted to know how to manage it properly. He had been working full-time as a teacher at a small school at Wheelwright, but he knew it was a vocation that would one day bore him. Coss had his father's curiosity and he needed more of a challenge.

Two hours later, father and son strolled right down to the job site. As good fortune would have it, the workers were having their lunch. Lische walked over to have a conversation with the men, but Coss was captivated by the steam engine. He peered into the firebox and examined the belts and pulleys.

The men explained to Lische that the railroad would one day come. Settlers were asking the state for an access road all the way to Prestonsburg. Settlers wanted land, and they wanted to build schools and shops. State officials were working with a large land development company, Collins and Mayo. This was all part of the Reconstruction Act. In return, Kentucky would have ongoing revenue in the form of property tax.

That evening at dinner, Coss was too excited to eat. He was alive with dreams and grandiose plans.

"Listen, Pop," he said. "This thing is huge, and we need to be a part of it. People will need all manner of things. First of all, we need to hire a land surveyor to section off building lots. We need more pasture land so we can raise more livestock. We can sell meat, milk, eggs, fruits, and vegetables. We'll make a handsome profit on it all."

Lische was never as excited as his son regarding money. Whenever such discussions arose, he would always ask, "Why should we work so hard for money we don't need?"

And Coss would always reply, "It's for the future, Pop."

Chapter Twelve

It was 1883, and twenty-three-year-old Coss had worked to clear bottom land for farming and other development. Settlers trickled into the area at a slow but steady pace, and Coss was there to provide for their needs. If they needed land to build on, he would sell small parcels. If they needed food, he could provide whatever was needed—for a fair price, of course. Coss also built a post office and became the area's first postmaster.

Most of the settlers came with large families, while others came to start new families. There were veterans from the war seeking a new life, and others who had heard stories of opportunity. There were the Newsomes, the Tacketts, the Mullens, and the Halls. Even two rivaling families moved to Weeksbury to forget the past and start anew: Enoch Hatfield with his wife and two sons, and William McCoy with his wife, son, and two daughters. There were those who fought for the Union and those who had fought for the South. But here, everyone lived quietly and in harmony.

Coss had a beckoning love for money, even though his father often reminded him of the scripture that states, 'For the love of money is the root of all evil.'

"We don't need money, Coss," Lische would scold. "Let those people keep their money. They've worked hard to earn it."

Coss would sneer and say, "If we don't need money, Pop, then they don't need it any more than we do. Remember one thing: you can trade for some things, but money buys everything."

Gold coins, silver coins, little by little, the money kept coming. Coss didn't trust banks, so he had his own hidden coffers.

He then convinced his father to assist him in clearing more land and building fences and barns. He wanted to invest in beef cattle and hogs to butcher and sell to the settlers.

Coss decided one day to hike through a low pass in the mountain already known as Lische Gap to visit their closest neighbor to the south. Their family had gotten to know the neighbor and his family. Many years ago, from high atop Collier Rock, Lische had watched the neighbor clear the land and build his cabin.

Massie Tackett was now a man in his forties, although a life of toil made him look much older. He had been pinned with the moniker Granny Tackett. He was a likable fellow and another source of information for Coss.

Coss spent long hours listening to the old frontiersman. When Massie had lived in Virginia, he had learned the trade of a wheelwright. Coss learned much from Massie. He learned to repair wheels, to make tools and furniture. Coss became complacent when Massie told wild stories of the days when he and Lische ran from the army or hid in caves. Coss wanted to learn things that he might one day use to make money. He listened intently to elders, but in his mind he was retaining what he thought to be valuable knowledge and discarded the rest.

It seemed that every settler who came had a different trade to share. There were coopers, who made barrels and buckets. There were millers, and gunsmiths and silversmiths. Although scattered and spread over a number of miles, a community was beginning to form. There was even a doctor not much more than ten miles away.

It was in 1883 that Coss met Frankie Jane Davis. Frankie was a simple lady, and not the prettiest girl he'd ever seen, but he was smitten. He visited her family on a daily basis in an effort to win their approval before asking her for courtship.

But after nearly six months of hanging around her family, doing chores and running errands, Frankie still didn't seem to notice Coss. His next strategy was to wheedle her person to person, but that didn't seem to work either. One day, he felt he had nothing to lose, so he asked her to come to dinner at his parents' home

She simply said, "Sure."

Within days, Coss was building a house; he was going to ask Frankie to marry him. And so he did.

She said, "Of course not."

Coss had already invested a great deal to win her favor, but he wasn't about to give up on Frankie. Now he needed another strategy. But the more he wanted her, the more she rejected him.

Coss remained patient and continued his wheedling until one day he convinced her to see the house he had built. It was a simple wooden structure with two bedrooms, a kitchen, and a sitting room. Nothing fancy, but the location was beautiful. The house sat at the base of the mountain with a grove of tall poplar trees to the west and leading up the mountain. The front of the house faced east, and there he had built a full-length porch. In the front yard stood a large buckeye tree and a large beech tree stood just on the other side of the creek that flowed through the yard. Fruit trees of all kinds had been planted by his father years ago and were now bearing cherries, apples, plums, and peaches.

"The house is no mansion," he said to her. "But I think we could be happy here and start a family. There's fresh water, and the mountains will block the wind. We have lots of room for gardening and pasture land for livestock. I built the porch so we could sit here and watch the sunrise—and the moon. I made this for us, Frankie."

He held his breath, for this would be his final effort.

Frankie pondered for a long time, and then she began to speak softly. "Coss, you know I'm only twenty years old. Until you came along, I hadn't even considered leaving home. I still feel like a child in so many ways." She paused. "I have thought about it a great deal, and I think you're a kind and gentle person, but if you're ever mean to me, then I'm going home."

Frankie's voice grew in volume. "And I want you to know I'm not an old-fashioned girl, Coss. I will not be your slave, nor will I be at your beck and call. This has to be a partnership, where decisions are made together. If you can accept those terms, then I'll marry you."

Coss let out a whooping yell, jumped up and down, and clapped his hands. Then he turned to her. "Soon, Frankie, soon. I want to spend Christmas here with you."

They were married on his father's birthday, 16 August 1884. On 29 November 1885, Coss and Frankie celebrated the birth of their first child. They named him Taube. Taube was the first of five children who were, as they say, 'stair-stepped' about eighteen months apart. After Taube, there was Floyd, Joe, daughter Dine, and Ben.

Coss continued to develop his entrepreneurship, making money at every opportunity. However, he also spent it at every opportunity. He invested just to invest. He bought high and sold low. Even though he was an expert in horses and other livestock, he purchased animals of poor breeding, banking on the hope that someone would come along and need the animals badly enough to pay an inflated price. This practice earned him a reputation that nearly destroyed his business. Coss did eventually learn from his father and became very cautious in purchasing livestock, especially horses.

As always, Lische often scolded his son. "You spend money faster than most folks can give it away."

"You're old-fashioned, Pop," Coss would say. "You're too old-fashioned, and you're too softhearted. You'd rather give something away than make a profit."

At that point, the discussion would usually end.

Chapter Thirteen

Coss shook his head in disbelief. A powerful thunderstorm had produced enough wind and hail to destroy his crops and most of the fruit harvest. It was July 1890. With very little left to sell, his income would be reduced considerably. He was well prepared for it, but still, it was a setback. A mistake he would not make again.

In January 1891, he visited each and every customer to announce he was getting out of the farming business. However, he would now lease choice lots near their homes so they could do their own gardening. His plan worked; hence, he increased his income and eliminated the financial risk of crop loss. That March, two men walked into the post office and asked where they might find Lische. Coss looked at the two men suspiciously.

"I'm not sure where he is at the moment," he said, "but I handle his affairs. I'm his son. My name is Cossburg."

One of the strangers cleared his throat, and then he spoke. "Well, sir, we were told to speak directly to the land owner. My name is Ben Soble, and this is Seth Harris. We represent Collins and Mayo."

"Follow the trail that leads east," Coss said. "Keep to the left, and that will lead you to my father's place. Be there at four p.m."

Ben said, "But, sir, that's four hours from now. Can't we see him now?"

"No," Coss replied. "I'm not available till then. As I said, I handle my father's affairs."

At four p.m. sharp, the two men dismounted in front of Lische's cabin. Introductions were made.

Again, Ben was the first to speak. "Sir, we represent a rather large land development company, DBA Collins and Mayo of Pittsburgh. I guess the only way to do this is to get right to the matter." He paused. "We would like to purchase your timber."

"I see," Lische said. Then he added, "Would you gentlemen join us for dinner?"

Ben said, "Well, we're both hungry, but are you sure your missis won't be put out? We wouldn't want to impose. Perhaps she's not prepared for company."

"Sir, my wife is always prepared for company," Lische replied.

With that, the four men walked into the cabin, where Sally was already placing dinner on the table. Lische invited them to sit.

"Gentlemen, we'll have our meal, and then we'll talk business."

They enjoyed roast beef, new potatoes, corn, green beans, and fresh-baked bread. Dessert was a cobbler made with wild raspberries. The men continually praised Sally's cooking throughout the meal. They both swore they hadn't had such a fine meal since they left Pittsburgh.

Lische then invited them to join his family on the front porch. He then said, "Now, sir, you were saying?"

"As I stated," Ben said, "we represent a land investment company from Pittsburgh. We would like to purchase the lumber sized timber from your land."

"From what section?" Lische asked.

Ben hesitated. "I'm afraid I don't understand."

"From what section?" Lische repeated. "I own just over fifty-three thousand acres."

Both men were agape. Ben said, "Sir, we were told you owned a lot of land, but I had no idea. Just over fifty-three thousand acres? Wow! Well, sir, I guess we would like to purchase the timber from the section closest to Martin."

Coss spoke up. "Well, we've never considered selling just the timber. We'll have to think about it for a few days and let you know."

"If you decide to sell," Ben said, "I'll have Seth here draw up a contract, as he's an attorney."

"That won't be necessary," Coss said. "We'll draw our own contract. In the meantime, you men can stay here for the night."

Lische and his family were kind and hospitable to the two men, but Coss couldn't wait for them to leave. The wheels of good fortune were spinning out of control in his head. He needed time alone with his father.

The men left early the next morning with a promise that Lische and Coss would have a proposal for them by the end of the following day. Coss and Lische watched as the men went out of sight, and then they joined Sally and Frankie on the porch.

"Listen, Pops—this is the chance of a lifetime. We can make a mint from this."

"I'm not sure we need a mint," Lische said. "And I'm even less sure I want to sell my timber. You realize that would render the land worthless."

"But, Pop, why have it if you can't make money from it? If we work this just right, we can sell the timber and still keep the land. The trees will grow back."

"Not in our lifetime. Forests like this take centuries to grow."

Coss turned to his mother for consensus. "Mother, what do you think?"

Sally said, "It's all up to you two. But be careful what you sign. We don't even know these men."

Coss said, "We're not going to sign their contract—they're going to sign ours. Pop, just let me draw up the contract, and then tell me what you think."

"All right, son," Lische said. "Draw it up." Coss ran home excitedly to start the contract. He worked long into the night but still had work to do the next morning. He asked Frankie to drop the children at his parents' place so she could look after the post office. By mid-afternoon, he approached his father with a contract that read as follows:

Now entering into a contract between the Johnson Land Company and Collins and Mayo Land Development Company. Signed before witnesses on this the ...... day of March in the year of our lord 1891. The purpose of this contract is to establish a clear and concise agreement between the two companies for the sale and processing of lumber. This said lumber shall be taken from the estate of Elisha Johnson. The entities bound in this contract shall be referred to as follows:

The Johnson Company as Seller and Collins and Mayo as Purchaser. The terms of this contract are as follows:

1. Purchaser shall provide all tools and equipment necessary for cutting and processing lumber.

2. Purchaser shall provide adequate draft animals.

3. Purchaser shall provide one steam-powered winch with two thousand feet of one-half-inch steel cable.

4. Purchaser agrees to allow Seller to purchase all tools and equipment on monthly terms with a maximum markup of ten per cent.

5. Purchaser shall pay in cash currency on the first day of each month at a rate of fourteen cents per board foot. One board foot is described as sawn from a log twelve inches long, twelve inches wide, and one inch thick un-planed.

6. If Purchaser defaults one term of this agreement, Seller shall have the right to take

possession, or dispose of all assets pertaining to this contract.

7. Seller shall provide and direct all manpower.

8. Seller shall deliver all finished goods to a central point to be determined and designated by both entities.

Signed
Purchaser..........................Date...............
Seller................................Date...............

Seth Harris swallowed hard when he read the terms of the contract. He just folded the paper, stuck it into his inside coat pocket, and said, "We'll have to contact our home office."

Two days later, the men met again with Lische and Coss.

Harris said, "We accept your terms, but we'll only pay twelve cents per board foot. The contract was signed, and the Johnsons were in the lumber business. The men said they would start sending in tools and equipment within ten days, and then they rode away.

When they were out of sight, Lische said to Coss, "I'm surprised you accepted a two-cent reduction in our price."

Coss said, "I'm surprised they didn't offer eight cents per foot."

"I have another question," Lische said. "Why are we financing tools and equipment? We have money—we could've paid cash for everything we need."

"Yeah, Pops, but why use our money? We're paying a ten per cent markup, but we're going to sell these tools to our workers with a twenty per cent markup."

Chapter Fourteen

There had been a great number of changes in the thirty-four years since Lische cleared a trail through this area. Lische had sold small parcels of land for a handsome profit. Many houses had sprung up along the banks of Beaver Creek. Lische knew most of the people. They appeared to be good, God-fearing people, and Coss was about to put them to work.

The day after Lische signed the contract with Collins and Mayo Coss got on his horse and went door to door looking for help. There were only two stipulations: the men had to be able-bodied, and they had to be willing to work ten hours a day, six days a week. He was looking for twenty men to start with. The rate of pay would be a dollar and twenty cents per day, including a midday meal.

Coss walked into a general store in Martin, where he had seen the finest in cooking stoves. He bought one for his mother and one for Frankie. He ordered a third stove and asked that it be delivered to his sawmill site. When it arrived, he chained it to a tree and hired two middle-aged women to cook. He wanted middle-aged women to ensure they were experienced enough to cook well. They would be paid eighty cents per day, including their meals. They were also allowed to take any leftover perishables home to their families.

Lische continued to take his early-morning strolls. He hadn't seen the guardian in years, but since signing the contract, he had seen it daily. It became clear to him that the spirit was not happy. That worried Lische a great deal.

On 10 April 1891, the first of many centuries old trees crashed to the ground along the south bank of Left Beaver Creek. It would take another three days to set up the steam-powered equipment, but it would be ready when the first logs were pulled in. However, that was just about the time when the spring rains set in.

So much went wrong in those first few weeks. Lische was sure there was a curse. The steam-powered winch, which was shackled to a large tree, could only chug and groan as it struggled to pull large logs through the mud. Workhorses sometimes sank a foot and a half in the mud. The entire work site became mire. In the third week of operation, a widow-maker branch ripped from a falling tree, crushing a man's legs. His wounds slowly healed, but he never returned to the job. And although all workers were instructed to wear protection on their legs, one man was bitten by a rattlesnake just above the top of his shoe. The man lived, but almost lost his leg. It was months before he was able to return to work.

But in spite of all the difficulties, the work continued. The site received orders for various sizes of lumber in increments of ten thousand board feet per order. Long before the crew could fill an order, they'd receive another in the mail.

As the days passed, things began to operate more smoothly. Two heavy spring wagons hauled large stacks of lumber to a yard in Martin, where it was sorted and stacked to dry. Softwood logs were used for siding and shingles, while hardwood was sawn for timber columns, floor joists, and rafters. Much like an assembly line, the lumber moved in perpetual motion, the forest began to recede, and the money started pouring in.

Coss worked long hours—never resting, always running here and there, and trying to manage every aspect of the entire operation. Word spread about the work. Each day, new men gathered at what was called the boss barn, asking to be hired. Coss handled all the hiring, but there was very little firing, for every man was needed. Coss had a rather unusual way of selecting workers. He always said he could tell just from a man's handshake or the way he walked whether he was worthy of a day's wages. The workforce continued to grow as more orders and money rolled in.

Coss couldn't have been happier with the two women doing the cooking. They started their day at six a.m. sharp and started serving at eleven thirty. It soon became obvious that one stove was not enough, so a second was added. They roasted entire sections of beef and pork. Whole chickens were slow-roasted over a bed of coals. Fresh fruits and vegetables were brought in daily from family farms. About an hour before the meal was to be served, the smell of baking bread pervaded over the smell of sawdust.

Tables and benches were quickly assembled from rough-sawn lumber. It was hard to keep track of the growing crew, but they knew some men showed up to eat even though they were not part of the workforce. Coss never made a point of identifying the freeloaders; he didn't like to see anyone go away hungry. Other non-employees showed up and asked if they could pay for a meal—they were charged five cents.

In 1900, Lische celebrated his sixtieth birthday. He was now a wealthy man. Although he had added on to his cabin and took for himself some of the finer things in life, he had never really changed. His habits were the same. He planted his garden in the spring and gathered fruit from trees he had planted years before. He still loved to stroll through the forest and watch the seasons change. And of course, there was always his morning face-washing.

He often scolded Coss that he should be careful not to become greedy. He also warned him not to work his life away and neglect his family. Lische worried that Coss was moving at such a pace that a stumble would result in a disastrous fall.

But Coss ignored his father's warnings. He kept expanding, growing, and staying ever on the lookout for a bargain. On one hand, he was a very generous man to anyone deserving. On the other hand, he hated laziness. He was even known to flog a man who refused to carry his weight.

One day, Coss rode through the area and noticed some items were missing. Coss hired an armed guard and ordered him to shoot to kill anyone caught stealing. The guard was to walk his post from eight thirty p.m. to four thirty a.m.

"But what about the hours before eight thirty p.m. and after four thirty a.m.?" someone asked him.

Coss said, "The average thief does his dirty work in the dead of night. He's certainly too lazy to get up early in the morning to steal." After that, nothing else was taken from the job site.

In fact, the crime rate in the entire area decreased dramatically around that same time. By the turn of the century, the community had grown. A school, a church and even a jail had been built. Folks in the area were just as proud of their jail as they were of the new school and church. The jail was nothing more than a concrete box with absolutely no comforts to speak of. When construction was completed, they had an open house. It was immediately clear to any would-be criminal that this was no place to end up.

Coss's operation had created so many jobs it had a positive effect on the entire population of southeast Kentucky. In some cases, two or more members of a household worked for his company. When people gathered for church services on Sunday, the transformation was obvious. They no longer looked like the sad, hungry and beleaguered people of the frontier. They appeared healthy, well dressed and happy. They arrived in well-kept buggies or wagons.

Coss and his family enjoyed great prosperity as well. It was once rumored that Coss bragged that he had money to burn. The rumor went on to claim that he proved his point by lighting a cigar with a twenty-dollar bill. Those who knew him never believed such a tale to be true. Coss was far too intelligent to do such a thing—and Lische would certainly never have allowed such foolhardy behavior.

Taube turned fifteen in 1900. Every moment when he could escape school, he stayed on his father's heels. Although Coss denied it, people often said he favored Taube over his other children. Nevertheless, he taught Taube diligently and allowed him to sit in on important meetings. Taube never asked questions. He only listened and learned the ways of business.

Chapter Fifteen

The country went through decades of reconstruction after the Civil War, and this era merged directly into a marvelous industrial boom. By the turn of the century, long trainloads of coal were pouring out of the mountains of Virginia, West Virginia, and Kentucky. It was as if the nation was hungry and eating itself.

Day and night, trains loaded with coal headed for blast furnaces in cities such as Ironton in Ohio, Pittsburgh, Cleveland, and Detroit. Coal was also being used to power steam engines for generating electricity. Shrouds of smoke and fog—soon to be called smog—hung over large cities. It was a time of invention, of creation and excitement. The entire nation was moved and pushed onward ahead of it.

In the spring of 1901, Coss heard a rumble to the west. It almost sounded like thunder, but there wasn't a cloud in the sky. A short time later, he heard the sound again. He got on his horse and started in the direction of the sound.

After nearly an hour's ride, he came into a long, narrow clearing that seemingly had no end. He continued on to where he saw smoke and dust rising and heard the sound of machinery.

It didn't take long to realize the railroad was coming.

Coss continued along the construction area to a rather elaborate railcar. He asked to speak to the men in charge and was surprised to see Ben Sobel and Seth Harris. After a short greeting, they introduced him to Charles Osmand, who represented Chesapeake and Ohio (C&O) Railroad.

They told Coss of their intention to build a railroad to the headwaters of every creek and stream. The purpose was to extract coal from the mountains and build communities. The grandiose plan would include the land now owned by one Lische Johnson.

The men wanted to have a meeting with Lische to discuss the sale of his property to Collins and Mayo. Coss indicated he was very doubtful of his father's willingness to sell, but they still wanted the meeting. Of course, Coss himself saw nothing but money for his family and wonderful growth and improvements for the area.

Coss and Frankie had dinner with his parents that night. He introduced them to a new soft drink known as Coca-Cola. Lische went on and on about the pleasant taste of the beverage and said he would ask the merchant to stock it for him.

This led Coss into his long, rehearsed, and convincing speech about all the wonderful things to come as the times changed. Carefully he worked in the subject of selling their land to Collins and Mayo.

Lische could see the excitement in his son's eyes, but he had never once considered selling his land. He stood up, walked a few paces, and then turned back to Coss.

"No, Cos, absolutely not."

The next day, Coss returned to the fancy railcar with the news.

"Coss, you have to convince him to at least meet with us," Ben said.

"Well, I still have my doubts," Coss replied, "but I'll ask him again in a few days."

Ben said, "We don't have a few days—we have coal to mine and houses to build."

"Listen," Coss said. "I know my father. If you push him, you'll never get any cooperation out of him."

So Coss waited three days before he approached his father again. This time, he beseeched his father to at least meet with the men and hear what they had to say. Lische finally agreed, but he made it clear he was making no promises regarding the outcome of the meeting.

Two days later, Coss led the three businessmen to Lische's cabin. As before, Lische insisted they have dinner before any business was discussed. And after the meal, Lische insisted that Sally, Frankie and Taube be allowed to take part in the discussion.

Lische said to the three gentlemen, "Tell me exactly what your intentions are, should I sell to you this land."

As usual Ben was the first to speak. "Well, sir, it's rather complicated. How much time will you give me to make my case?"

Lische said, "You can go on forever if you can interest me in what you're saying."

Ben set his bottle of Coke on the porch banister, cleared his throat, and said, "I'm going to give it to you straight, Lische. Our main purpose is to extract and sell coal on the open market. We've been at this for some time. In doing so, we've made a very lucrative profit. We don't deny it. But at the same time, we've built entire towns and communities. It's a large plan, but I'll tell some of the highpoints of it.

Lische nodded for Ben to continue. "The first stage is to get the railroad built and coal mines opened. Small ponies will be used to pull buggies loaded with coal out of the mines until a power plant can be built. Then the ponies will be replaced by electric engines running along a small rail system. Remember—having a power plant means substations will be built and electricity will be provided to every home for those who want it.

"We'll also be putting up hundreds of new homes with a central water supply. At the junction of the hollows two miles west of here, we're going to build an office building, a general store, a soda fountain, and a theater. We'll also develop two recreational parks for adults and two playgrounds for children.

"So you see, Mr. Johnson, this is a good thing for everyone. I should also mention that at our company store, we will have on hand the finest in merchandise. The most-modern tools and gadgets for your home, the latest in fashion, and the freshest groceries brought in on the train each day. Working men can purchase anything in this store on credit with nothing more than a signature."

Lische gazed out at the creek rushing by the cabin. "Well, sir," he said, "I had no intentions of building a town when I came here to stake my claim. Most people like me are seeking privacy when they move into remote areas such as this. However, that was a long time ago, and things change. But needless to say, I'll have to think about this for a couple of days."

Lische started to turn away, but then he turned back.

"I have one question: What if I say no?"

This time it was Seth Harris who spoke. "We'll take the coal anyway. You see, there's a saying in our business: 'The meek shall inherit the earth but not the mineral rights.' We will simply tunnel under your property from every direction and take the coal right out from under you. These beautiful creeks and springs will be drained from deep below the surface, and you'll have no water. On the other hand, if you sell to us, we will install a water system for everyone.

"I don't see how you could possibly refuse. The country needs this coal for heat, for electricity, and to make steel. We need this coal, and we're going to take it. Be reasonable, Mr. Johnson. We're willing to offer you a fair price."

"And what would that fair price be?" Coss asked.

Harris said, "Well, considering that a lot of the timber is gone, I would say about forty cents per acre."

From the look Lische gave this man, Coss and Taube were sure he would flog him. Instead, Lische cleared his throat and said calmly, "Gentlemen, you may go to hell."

As the men rode away, Lische turned to Coss. "You better look into this matter and find out if what the attorney said about mineral rights is true. But in the meantime, we're not going to waste time worrying about it."

The fact is, Lische did worry about a great deal.

Chapter Sixteen

Lische had a long, sleepless night. He thought about what he had sacrificed to claim this land, to clear it, and to tame it. He had always known the day would come when he would have to meet a challenge such as this one. He needed time to think, and there was no place like Collier Rock to do it.

First he would have breakfast with Coss and Taube. He had to at least pretend not to be worried. But when they arrived, it was obvious they hadn't slept well either.

Coss was the first to speak. "You know, Pop—this might not be such a bad thing. We have money now, and if we sell, we'll have even more. You could buy any place you like. You and Ma would never have to worry about anything as long as you live."

Lische said, "We don't worry about anything now. And we have our home." He shook his head. "It's just too sudden. I'll have to think about it."

Coss and Taube left for work. Lische kissed Sally on the cheek and told her he would be back in a few hours. Then he washed his face in the creek and forgot about his anger.

He set out along an old, familiar path, as he had done for more than forty years. He had walked this path during times of worry and stress. He had also walked it during times of happiness. But this time was different. His mind had never been as mixed up as this.

He was sure the guardian would appear today. He hoped it would. Although he had never communicated with it before, perhaps he could glean some kind of message from it on this day.

His sixty-first birthday would be here soon, and that was something else to consider. It was a reminder that the time would come when he would have to relinquish all business dealings to Coss. But not yet. Sure, he had a stiff back from time to time and a little soreness in the hips. But aside from that, he was completely healthy. In fact, he had just reached the low pass that carried his name: the Lische Gap. Most folks wouldn't be able to make it to this point, but he wasn't even out of breath.

Lische paused only to look back over his domain, then he turned left and started up the steep ridgeline toward Collier Rock. From here, Lische could see the plateau towering above the mountaintop in the midmorning sun.

A half hour later, he stood atop the cliff. Somehow it made him feel welcome. He walked to what he called his eastern lookout and sat down. He breathed in the fresh mountain air and the sweet smell of pine needles drying in the warm sun. He looked out over familiar mountain peaks and the morning fog as it dissipated near the valley floor far below. Here there was no trouble, no problems to solve, and nothing but proof of God's wisdom. There was nothing more soothing to a troubled mind than God's handiwork.

Lische sat there for hours, trying to solve these unexpected problems that had him so confused. He didn't like this fellow, Seth Harris. He surely didn't trust him. But Lische was afraid the man was right. When Lische first registered his claim, there was no mention of his procuring the mineral rights as well. He had never heard of such a thing. Until recently, no one even knew there were valuable minerals underground.

Lische leaned back on the soft blanket of pine needles and realized how little sleep he had gotten the night before. Soon he was fast asleep.

Before he knew it, he was suddenly awakened by a rush of air across his face, as if a large bird had zipped past. He didn't bother to look; he knew it was the guardian.

"Welcome, old friend," he said. "I'm sure I know how you feel about my dilemma. I only wish you could tell me how to solve it."

He closed his eyes and felt the sensation again, but he still didn't stir. However, when the guardian passed him a third time, Lische finally stood up. He stood up and walked over to his western lookout.

It was then that Lische realized what the guardian had been trying to tell him. Storm clouds stretched along the western horizon as far as he could see to the south and as far as he could see to the north. He now knew the guardian was trying to warn him. Everything happens for a reason, whether its fate or divine providence, there are warning signs if we learn to recognize them.

Lische had to stay and determine how fast the storm was moving and how bad it would be. The only way to understand the weather is to be on a mountaintop. From deep in the hollows or valley floors, you can only see the sky directly above. However from the mountaintop, you can see for countless miles in every direction.

Lische checked his pocket watch—it was two fifteen. He would wait twenty minutes to see what happened next. Lische estimated the storm to be about a hundred miles away. Very slowly but surely, it was moving ever closer. It appeared to be growing stronger as the clouds kept getting darker.

Lische had seen only one storm that looked like this, and that storm nearly took his farm in a flash flood. Lische had seen that one coming as well, but he didn't do anything to prepare for it. And it almost ended in tragedy.

He suddenly had an epiphany—there was a deeper meaning in all this, there was a message.

His thoughts went back to that storm so many years ago. He thought about how he had sat safe and dry in his cave, ignoring all the signs that should have been obvious to him. He remembered how all of nature became a merciless monster. Like a creature with many tentacles, it reached out as the small mountain streams flooded together, flushing and folding everything in the path. And Lische had carelessly aided the monster: one log and some debris that he should have cleared from the creek bed was all the monster needed.

Lische jumped up and looked around him. He saw a large pine branch slowly dip under an invisible weight. He waved to it. The branch lifted slowly back into place, as if the weight had left. He then felt a rush of air across his face. Somehow he knew the guardian was gone forever.

Lische had got a message from it after all—more of a message than he had ever hoped for. There was no need—and no time—to reflect. His mind was clear.

The storm was approaching, but this time he would be ready. He had things to do. Cossburg's crew had been cutting timber along the creek banks. There was lots of brush in the path of the storm.

As he raced down the mountain, Lische felt elated. Plans and ideas were flying past him. As fast as he could process one, another would enter his brain.

The first order of business was to make a way for the monster. That meant clearing debris in the path of the impending flash flood. But it also meant making a way for Collins and Mayo. He would grant them a right of way for their railroad and limited access to open coal mines, but he would keep his land for now. That was what the guardian had directed him to do.

When Lische reached the house, he immediately threw a saddle on his horse and raced off to find Coss and Taube. Along the way, he summoned men to the lumberyard. Taube had just arrived from school. Both he and Coss looked troubled as they saw Lische galloping toward them. They knew something was very wrong—or very right.

Lische didn't waste any time. He gave orders to drop everything, gather more men, and start clearing brush and debris from the banks of the main creek. The storm would soon be upon them, within no more than two hours.

The crew got to work. As soon as the cloud appeared, Lische instructed the workers to rush home to their families.

"Coss," Lische said, "you gather up your family and come over to our place for dinner. Be prepared to spend the night."

Coss and Taube gave him a puzzled look.

Coss and his family arrived at five thirty p.m.—just after the first rumble of thunder. They quickly assembled for dinner. Lische stood at the end of the table with Sally to his right; Coss stood at the other end with Frankie to his right. Taube and Floyd stood at one side of the table, while Joe and Ben stood on the other. Little Dine sat at her small play table in the corner. Lische led the family in a short prayer of thanks, and then they were seated.

They made lighthearted conversation as they ate, but spoke nothing of business. That was probably the reason they all rushed through the meal.

With the meal out of the way, the men headed to the front porch to watch the storm and talk business. Sally and Frankie started gathering the dishes, but Lische said, "No. The workday is over. What has to be discussed concerns us all. Please join us on the porch."

It was a full two hours before dusk, but the sky was completely dark. The rain was steadily increasing. There was thunder and lightning but not much wind.

There was a long silence until Coss finally spoke. "Are you worried about Collins and Mayo, Pop?"

"No, not anymore," Lische said. "I don't care for those men, but I don't think they'll go away. I don't intend to sell to them at this time, but I'll grant them leave to build their railroad. Provided they pay for the easements, I'll allow 'em to open a limited number of coal mines. We will draw up agreements for these rights, and they'll be given only under my hand. Any questions so far?"

Coss let out a long exhale. "I'm just glad you're willing to work something out with them, Pop. Word got around that you were preventing the railroad and the other development. A lot of people were getting sore."

"I'm not the least concerned about who's sore. My brothers and I came here years before any of 'em. We fought the weather, snakes, and the wild animals to settle this land. When a man does that, he reserves certain rights." Lische nodded to himself. "So invite those Collins and Mayo men to dinner on Wednesday, and we'll discuss it. And Coss, I want you and Taube to discuss this and draw up some contracts—and remember who you're representing."

Little Ben, who was always quiet by nature, said in a low voice, "We should make a bank and make those bad men put their money into it."

"Shh!" Frankie said. "Be quiet, Ben. The men are talking."

"What did you say?" Lische asked.

"I just told him to be quiet and not interrupt," Frankie said.

"No—not you, Frankie. I want Ben to stand up and repeat what he said," Lische said. "This is why I wanted the entire family involved in this discussion. Now, Ben, I want you to repeat what you said."

"We should make a bank and make those bad men put their money into it," Ben repeated.

"That's brilliant, son. Come here and sit close to me, and we'll make a plan." As Ben climbed onto his grandfather's lap, Lische said to Coss, "Well, what do you think?"

"I think it's a great idea, Pop. Taube and I will get started on it as soon as we finish the contracts."

With the business issues out of the way, the family just sat on the porch, watching the rain and the ever rising creeks until it was time to turn in for the night. A steady downpour lasted until long after midnight.

It was another sleepless night for Lische, Coss, and Taube. But tonight they were wide awake with excitement. They lay in bed listening to the rain and the creeks.

The storm wasn't as bad as Lische had expected. Still, clearing the brush from the creek had definitely averted disaster.

Chapter Seventeen

Day and night, the railroad pushed deeper into the mountains. Most people call them train cars, but in the coal industry they are called coal guns. In the beginning, all the coal guns were painted black with C&O in white on the side. Soon, however, there were other names on the coal guns, as other large coal companies arrived for a piece of the treasure. It was as if these mountains were providing for the entire nation's need.

After Collins and Mayo, other companies began to arrive. There was Inland Steel, Copper State, Bethlehem Steel, and Island Creek. These companies also came with grandiose plans for eastern Kentucky. They knew they would ravage the land, so these plans were only frail attempts at making things right with the landowners.

Just like Collins and Mayo, the other large companies came in flashing money and making promises. They came complete with everything but manpower. They began to recruit members of Coss's workforce, and there was little he could do about. They were bleeding his company, but he would bleed theirs in return.

On the Wednesday following the storm, the men from Collins and Mayo once again had dinner with the Johnson family. After dinner, they assembled on the front porch, where Coss laid out the terms of the new contract. Lische himself had not seen the terms of the deed until then, but he had the utmost confidence in Coss.

Lische would issue a one-hundred-year lease on a strip of land fifty feet wide and approximately eighteen miles long. The route would begin at a point now known as Price, Kentucky, running east along the main creek. The route was not bound to one side or the other, thus giving the railroad the freedom to choose the path of least resistance. The contract mentioned four places where the road could split in order to gain access to the hollows known as Leagon, Jacks Creek, Wheelwright, and Caleb Fork.

C&O would be permitted to vary from the creek's right of way in order to blast tunnels through two mountains. The first would be one-quarter mile east of Leagon; the other would be .6 miles east of Melvin. The railroad would be obligated to build two passenger depots. The first depot would be located near the main junction at Wheelwright; the other would be at the main junction at the entrance of Caleb Fork.

In return for the easement, all wood products for the projects would be purchased from Coss's lumber mill. This included but was not limited to all railroad ties and bridge timbers. Lische would also grant them easement to open seven horizontal mine shafts, and Coss would provide the timbers for those as well. There was one final condition in the agreement: C&O would provide two flat cars to carry lumber from the Johnson lumberyard to a kiln near Paintsville. The wood products would be transported once a week free of charge for a full five years.

The Collins and Mayo men had come prepared for more of a confrontation—they didn't expect an agreement to be reached this easily. They took the contract, looked it over, then walked to the far side of the yard for privacy.

What did you think of the contract, Pop?" Coss asked once the men were out of earshot.

"Son, I'm just glad you're on my side," Lische replied.

When the men returned, they were ready and willing to sign.

With the contract completed, Lische said, "Now, gentlemen, how about a shot of brandy?"

The men looked at each other with total confusion. Ben said, "Lische, I thought we'd be the last people you'd want to drink with."

"What makes you think that?"

"Well, the other day, you told us to go to hell."

"That was then. Today is a different day," Lische said. "One thing for you to remember, gentlemen—never hold a grudge in business."

"One thing for *you* to remember, sir," Ben said. "We work for a very persistent company—they'll keep after you for this land."

Chapter Eighteen

The next day, Lische instructed Coss to ride into Martin and Prestonsburg with Taube. They were to locate businessmen with enough capital to help sponsor a bank. Lische wanted to hold one million dollars in reserve.

It was very unusual for Coss to question his father, but this time he did. "Pop, we have enough money to fund this on our own."

"There are a number of reasons for having partners in a venture such as this," Lische said. "First of all, it keeps us from putting all our eggs in one basket. The second, bringing in partners means an instant customer base. In other words, these businessmen will bring their customers to our door. Third, they'll also bring us their expertise. Let's face it—we'll be new in the banking business." He continued, "However, we will maintain fifty-one percent of the ownership, and that gives us total control."

By the middle of 1903, the lumber business was beginning to wane. The demand was still strong, but the timber that remained was deep in the mountains and difficult to harvest.

There was a greater problem; manpower was getting harder to find and even harder to keep. The large coal companies were stealing Coss's workers faster than he could hire them. It wasn't because they offered higher wages. Rather, they simply convinced men that mining jobs would be more stable and predictable. Their hiring pitch was: "The weather never changes in the coal mine. It's fifty-five degrees all year round."

It didn't take Lische and Coss long to figure out how the big companies were able to keep their workforce: they allowed the men and their families to sink into abysmal debt at their company store. They kept in stock every new and shiny item one could imagine—everything from horseshoes to china cabinets. There was always something new to fit any family's needs, and they could get it with nothing more than a stroke of a pen. They also made sure there was no competition for miles.

The banking business was doing well, but Coss called for a meeting with the board of directors and it was to take place at Lische's cabin in one week. However, Lische was unaware of the reason for the meeting.

"I just hope it's important," Lische said. "Some of these men have to travel a long way."

"I'll try to make it worth their trouble, Pop." Coss replied.

In fact, Coss asked the men to bring along their families because he had planned a feast as well. Coss instructed Joe and Floyd to gather lots of dry hickory wood. The boys were told to prepare themselves to slaughter a 250-pound pig and six young hens for the business banquet.

People started arriving early on the day of the meeting. Counting the wives and children, there were thirty-six people in all. Each wife carried with her some kind of dish to share. There was hardly a need for introductions; the women immediately mingled together like family.

The food would not be ready for several hours, so Coss asked Lische if he could proceed as soon as all the partners were gathered together. When all the men were seated, Coss stood up and thanked them for coming.

"Gentlemen, we don't normally discuss business on an empty stomach, but today's a little different," Coss continued. "As most of you know, we've been losing manpower to these big coal companies for some time now. They're giving these men credit at their store, keeping them in debt, and thereby binding them to their jobs. It would take some of these men years to pay for things they've bought. Some of the families have purchased goods they simply can't afford.

"What I propose is to drop our interest rate two percent below what they're charging. We'll lend money to these people so they can go anywhere they want to spend it. They can get on the train and go to Lexington, for that matter. It's kind of a low blow, but it's the only way I know of striking back."

As the men were all shuffling and mumbling about, Benjamin Archer, of Prestonsburg, stood up. He waved his fist into the air and shouted, "I think it's goddamn brilliant! Now, when do we eat? I'm starving!"

With the business matters already out of the way, they opened a bottle of wine and Lische called for a toast to the families. Dinner was served at four p.m. Many of the guests said they had never seen such a feast. After dinner, the men, once again, gathered on the front porch but this time to drink brandy and smoke cigars. The women chatted as they put things away and overfed children lay snoozing in the shade of a poplar tree.

The lower interest rate proved to be a success. The number of credit accounts dropped at the company store so much, that six months later, Collins and Mayo were willing to compromise. They had two terms that would help the bank, as well as their store. The first term was that anyone who wanted to purchase on credit would be directed to get financing from the

Johnson Bank. The other term was an offer to let the bank handle the Collins and Mayo payroll.

The community was growing in leaps and bounds. Everywhere was the smell of fresh-cut wood and the sound of hammers and saws. A black man by the name of Odell Geats and his teenage son had been working for the lumber mill for just over a year. Coss noticed that they produced more than any crew on the job. So, Coss established a piece rate for them; therefore, they were able to make more money than the other crews. This created some animosity among the workers, but not much was ever said. You see, Geats had a secret. A secret recipe, that is. He made the best homemade liquor around. If he knew you, you could buy on credit.

One of Geats' longtime customers was Thomas Osborn. Osborn was said to have been a schoolyard bully type. He was one of those people everyone loved to hate. He had been thumped a couple of times, but that only made him meaner. He was also known for carrying a loaded pistol in his belt.

In mid-afternoon on a sunny Sunday, Osborn went to the Geats' home for whiskey. The rumor was that he had not paid his bill for some time and Geats refused to sell him anymore. The two men got into a scuffle and Geats somehow ended up with Osborn's gun. At near point-blank range, Geats shot Osborn just above the bridge of his nose.

The shot should have dropped that man on the spot, but it didn't. Osborn turned and stumbled about fifty yards before he dropped to his knees. He fell forward with his forehead resting on his right arm.

People had heard the shot and came out running from every direction.

You can hardly blame a man for defending his home. Though it was the gruesomeness to follow that was disturbing to folks. You see, it took Osborn a full twelve minutes to die. Onlookers knew there was nothing to be done, so they just stood there and wished him to die. Finally, after twelve minutes, with blood flowing from his nose and mouth, he gave out a loud gurgling gasp and died.

Soon the constable arrived. He took one look at the angry mob that had formed and wanted no part of it. He quickly turned his horse around and rode away.

In the meantime, Geats and his son had retreated into the house, refusing to come out. The mob gathered on the hill above Geats' house, demanding he surrender. Geats refused.

The townspeople grew angrier and some became violent. Geats had two mules, hogs, and some chickens in a fenced area, all were shot dead. Then a rock was thrown at the house; which led to frenzy. The stoning continued and by midnight, not a windowpane was left unbroken.

Shortly after, Geats emerged in the full moonlight with a white rag tied to a broomstick, asking for a truce. He told the mob that if they would leave him alone until daylight, he would pack up and leave. A man's voice shouted over the angry mob exclaiming, "Leave NOW Geats! No packing! No waiting!". To show they meant business, they threw a stick of dynamite which exploded just behind the house. The same man yelled out again threatening the next stick will be thrown down the chimney (which was in the center of the house).

With nothing more than the clothes on their backs, Odell Geats and his son surrendered and walked away in the middle of the night, never to be seen again.

Chapter Nineteen

Ben Sobel had been right. Collins and Mayo never stopped asking Lische to sell them his land. The nation was like a growing teenage boy who couldn't get enough to eat. His upkeep was expensive, and he was outgrowing his clothes faster than he could learn.

It was spring 1905, the world was changing by the hour. Large industrial cities were popping right up out of the cornfields. Gasoline powered engines were replacing steam and horses. There were all types of new gadgets. The greatest marvel of them all was when two brothers from Ohio invented a flying machine.

For Lische, it started out as a beautiful day in April, but it didn't end that way. Sally was a quiet woman by nature, though, after nearly a half century of marriage, Lische knew when something was wrong. They had an early breakfast and walked out to a small knoll not far from the back of the house. This was their spot. They didn't share it with anyone. They had a couple of homemade wooden chairs where they would sit for hours just listening to the birds.

After sitting for a bit, Sally suddenly turned to Lische. "You know," she said, "I'm not feeling well. I think I might go back to bed for a nap. I'm sure I'll feel better if I just rest a bit."

However, when she stood up, she almost fainted. Lische took her arm and helped her to bed.

Evening came, and she was still in bed. Lische wanted to send for the doctor, but Sally refused. By midnight, she was hot with fever but said she was cold. It was a time when people thought cold air caused illness, so Lische bundled her under heavy quilts.

At first light, Lische summoned Taube and told him to rush to Wheelwright for a doctor. After seeing Taube off, Lische returned to the cabin and rushed to her side—but Sally was already gone.

Coss and Frankie got there just minutes later and found Lische completely speechless. They knew Sally had passed.

Taube arrived with a doctor by the name of Circles. The doctor examined Sally and said he was sure pneumonia had taken her. Late that afternoon, the undertaker came and took her body to prepare it for burial. Lische was in no state of mind to help with the arrangements, so Coss and Frankie followed along in a buggy.

Taube stayed with Lische, but Lische was unable to speak. He just walked to the barn, got some digging tools, and started digging Sally's grave. The grave was dug on the little knoll where she loved to sit.

Nothing was ever the same after that day. The world had completely changed its physical appearance for Lische. Even his morning splash in the creek would not erase his pain. Nothing could give him a new outlook on life. His Sally was gone. Nothing seemed to matter anymore. Nothing had value, and no goals were worth achieving.

Lische could not sleep in his cabin. He spent a few nights with Coss and Frankie, but otherwise he roamed the wilderness. For almost two months, he wandered, lost and confused.

In June 1905, he instructed Coss to draw up a sales agreement. He only had two stipulation: One, the hollow where his and Coss's cabins stood would be leased and not sold. The lease would stand for one hundred years and consist of 280 acres. Furthermore, as long as his bloodline existed, his descendants would be allowed to remain there. Two, it was also stipulated that seven acres surrounding Sally's grave would be reserved as a cemetery for the Johnson family and their friends and neighbors.

In July, Coss acted under power of attorney for Lische. Just over 53,000 acres were sold for $26,830.

Lische soon moved out of the hollow and into the cabin his brother Harvey had built so many years before. He continued his journeys to Collier Rock; however, he avoided passing his old cabin. He couldn't bear the thought or the image in his head of his lovely wife. It almost killed him. He had approached the cabin once and there, as clear as day, sat his Sally in her favorite chair on the porch. He smiled at her memory but then as he passed, all happy thoughts left him as he took in the sadness and the loneliness of her grave.

Coss, too, had a lot of problems after the passing of his mother. He would stop by the post office or the bank, but he never cared to work the long hours he had in the past. He and his father were wealthy men, but wealth didn't seem to matter anymore. They quickly realized, how everything in life could lose its meaning.

Lische spent his days roaming the mountains, sometimes on foot and sometimes on horseback. It was late November 1905 and Lische sat staring eastward at an almost full moon rising above the mountains. The sun was already gone and he knew he should be making his way down the mountain, but Collier Rock was his favorite place to be alone. *So many changes I have seen since I settled here nearly a half century ago*, he said to himself. Far below Collier Rock was a well-traveled road, winding alongside Long Fork Creek. Houses now stood along the road and although it was nearly a mile away, he could see lights and hear the laughter of children as they played around a bonfire.

Blue smoke had settled near the valley floor as folks made fires for cooking evening meals and warming the autumn chill. The entire area now bustled with life and industry. A wagon came into sight on the Long Fork road with what looked to be a man and his family. They had no doubt been to the grocery store in Virgie. Seeing happy folks and children playing, sometimes made him feel sad and even more alone. Night was approaching quickly and Lische knew he should be on his way, but he so loved gazing at the stars and the smell of autumn. A breeze whispered through the pine trees, bringing back a memory of something his friend Massie had said while they were caught in a blizzard many years past; 'The wind blowing through pine trees is the coldest sound to be heard.'

It would be his first winter without Sally and he wasn't sure how he would make it through. For forty-seven years she had been a part of him.

At last, he stood up and walked toward his old hideout and onto the path leading home. It was dark and the moonlights glow began to erase the shadows of the mountains but Lische knew the route and worried very little about any wild animals, for most of them had been killed off or pushed out by settlers, therefore, he didn't carry a gun, only a walking stick. He decided not to take the short way home- that would mean passing the old cabin he and Sally built together. Instead, he continued following the path down into the low pass that now bears his name; Lische Gap. From there he would walk further west a mile to another low pass known as the John Gap. At that point, he would turn right and descend into Weeksbury.

He could see Massie Tackett's place and the glow of a warm fire through the windows. He knew his old friend was home with a full stomach, snug and happy with his wife, Polly. He paused for a moment on the gap to listen for any remaining crickets or frogs and breathe in the cool air, he hated to think of autumn slipping away. He wished he could go back in time and relive every minute with his Sally.

He tried not to glance down the hollow in the direction of his old cabin, for that would only bring him sorrow that he struggled to avoid. Suddenly, unsure of the reason, a foreboding force turned his gaze into the valley below where he saw a faint twinkle of light. He walked a few feet across the crest of the mountain for a better look. He just couldn't believe his eyes... The lantern signal swaying back and forth.

Without a second thought, Lische bolted headlong down the mountain toward the cabin, as flashing thoughts raced with him; could it be that he had been brought back in time? Could he finally be waking up from a long nightmare, or was he in fact having a dream at this moment? He didn't care. He didn't waste time trying to figure it out. Although it had been more than forty years since he had seen the lantern signal, he knew his Sally wanted him home and he was going to her.

Lische could have been seriously injured running down the mountain the way he had, but no thought of caution entered his mind. He finally stopped less than a hundred yards from his old home to stare over a dark dismal scene. The bright moon offered enough light to help him see the somber and lonely cabin. Unattended gardens stood in tall weeds now dead and dry. Unharvested corn hung from stalks and cucumbers lay rotting on the vine. There was no smoke from the chimney and no amber glow from the windows. But the most disheartening of the entire scene was the realization of Sally's grave.

Lische felt his strength leaving his body as his grip on the walking stick failed and his hands slid down; he fell to his knees and wept bitterly. There was no doubt in his mind he had seen the lantern but who could have played such a cruel joke? He took out a handkerchief to wipe his eyes and gather his thoughts. He had been through many hardships in his sixty-five years, but he was now being tested by some unexpected or evil force. Such a trick could have only been orchestrated by the Devil himself.

Lische finally regained enough strength to stand and look around him. Then he heard strange foreign sounds high above him. It was a sound unlike anything he had ever heard, unearthly and unholy. It was an evil cackling that flew in circles around the entire valley at an unbelievable speed. Something in his heart told him it was the Tempest that might one day carry him into Hell, but not tonight. Lische would not allow himself to be frightened. He thrusted his clinched fists into the air and shouted curses in defiance, then the sounds faded.

He walked to the little knoll and knelt at Sally's grave, but he could find no words for a prayer. He couldn't find a way to harvest the good and keep out the evil. He took his handkerchief; spread it on the head of Sally's grave and placed small stones at the corners to hold it in place. He then stood with a surrendering sigh and walked away in what remained of the evening light

Chapter Twenty

Coss had developed an eye for fine horses. He would get on the train and travel to Lexington or Louisville. There he found the finest of stock. He bought sleek black mares with straight backs and long legs. He bought the strongest of studs, and he began to produce beautiful colts to sell or trade. Taube had had a love for horses from the day he was born. He followed in his father's footsteps just to watch and learn.

As strange as it might seem, Coss and Frankie's five children didn't look alike, and they were as different in nature as night and day. Floyd and Joe delivered mail on horseback when they were old enough. However, they had no use for big business. They didn't dream of wealth nor did they seek it. They believed much in the way their grandfather believed and probably learned from him. Lische always believed that money would serve only to eventually enslave you. He always said, 'All a man needs is a small farm, some animals, and a good wife.' Joe and Floyd couldn't have agreed more.

They would play the game for now, but one day they would settle for a small patch of land; just enough to serve them.

Dine was a quiet little thing. Hours could pass, and you wouldn't know she was in the room. She married at a young age to a man by the name of Monk Hall. Monk had built a small house on the mountaintop and on the Floyd-Pike County line. They soon tried to start a family, but their first two children died just after birth. Their bodies were buried near their home.

Ben was different from all of them. He read pulp fiction and dime-store novels about the Old West. He called everyone 'partner' and walked around with a .44-caliber pistol strapped to his waist. He told everyone who would listen that he was heading out West to be a cowboy. No one believed him, but one day he left for Arizona and was never seen again.

By the year 1912, Collins and Mayo were operating a number of coal mines in the area. The railroad had been built into Weeksbury, and there was electricity. It appeared that Collins and Mayo had kept their word and were building everything they said would build.

Taube was probably the most educated man in the area, and Collins and Mayo had plans for him. The railroad came to a dead end at the mouth of the hollow where Lische tethered his horse during his first visit. Two brick buildings were built at the end of the railroad, one on each side. One would be used for storing supplies; the other was built to service mining equipment. Taube was hired to run the machine shop.

Taube probably saved a portion of every dollar he ever made. He knew a good bargain when he saw one, and he was always prepared. He had a motto that he followed carefully: get ahead and stay ahead. He would one day be resented for that fact.

As fate would have it, Taube met an enterprising young lady by the name of Ida Burk. They were married in 1912. They soon started their first business venture. They built a small stone building and leased it to the government as a post office for the community of Melvin. Also, there were a number of cars in the area and nowhere to buy gasoline. Taube and Ida saw the need and built a service station.

It was a time when most folks had gotten used to seeing new gadgets such as trains and motor cars, but not everyone. There were still some folks back in the hollows who had not yet seen an automobile. Such was the case with Marion Mullins and his wife, Ester. One day a salesman went bouncing up the rocky road leading to their cabin. Ester saw the car and shouted, "Lord have mercy, Pa, what is that thing coming up the road?" Marion picked up his shotgun, ran outside and shot the old car dead in the radiator. The man on the car jumped off and ran for his life. The old car drifted over into the ditch where it sat steaming. Marion walked back into the house and calmly stood the shotgun in the corner. His wife asked, "Did you kill that thing, Pa?"

Marion said, "No, but I made it turn that man loose."

Taube kept his job in the machine shop. He was well paid, and at the end of the day, he felt very fortunate to have spent his day in a warm, dry workplace. He watched as the men came out of those mines. He saw them grow old fast. They were black with coal dust and always wet, either from sweat or the water that almost constantly dripped from the roof of the mines.

Taube and Ida were happy but always striving for more. Then in 1913, Ida became pregnant. In the fall of that year, she gave birth to identical twins. They named them in honor of Taube's younger brothers, Joe and Floyd. Having children changed things but not much. Taube continued to work and to wheel and deal; while Ida stayed home taking care of the children and the bookkeeping.

Chapter Twenty-One

A single lady by the name of Ellen Hyden showed up one day in Weeksbury.

Ellen said she was from Pittsburgh and had come to town looking for work. She rented a small house in the section of Weeksbury known as Number One. (The coal surveyors had named the fast-growing neighborhood, and no one ever bothered to rename it.)

In her mid-twenties, Ellen was a buxom lady with long dark-brown hair. She was friendly enough, but she had a subtle way of letting everyone know she wanted to be left alone. With her was a small child named Tommy. People thought it strange that she was seldom seen with the child in public. It was almost as if he were a deep, dark secret. She said he was her little brother, but some people suspected he was her own child. She claimed her father had been killed in an industrial accident, and then her mother had abandoned her and Tommy. Ellen said she had not seen her mother in more than two years. She made no effort to hide her bitterness for her mother.

Soon after Ellen appeared, a young man named John Benson also showed up in Weeksbury. He was an attorney replacing Seth Harris, who had just retired from Collins and Mayo. John was from Pittsburgh as well. He said he was a single man fresh out of law school. Rumors soon circulated that there was a connection between John and Ellen from back in Pittsburgh, but they both denied it.

Perhaps the rumors brought Ellen to his attention, but John didn't waste any time pursuing her. Ellen ignored John for the longest time, but he was shameless in his attempt at courtship. Finally, one day she agreed to a short buggy ride with him. She refused him again for nearly a week, and then there was another ride. Soon there was a ride twice a week, and then it was almost every day.

I guess John never wondered why Ellen never permitted him to pick her up at her home. She always insisted on meeting him somewhere—the store, the post office, and so on. So he didn't know a thing about Tommy.

All Ellen said was that she had a secret, but she was not yet ready to share it with him.

"Is it a good secret or a bad one?" John asked, gently taking her hand.

Ellen looked away. "I don't think it's bad, but you might." She was clearly falling for him, but she was afraid of what he would think about Tommy being in her life.

Eventually they went away on the train for a three-day getaway for the Fourth of July. But as time wore on, John became more and more suspicious of whatever dark secret Ellen wouldn't share with him. John made every attempt to convince her that nothing—no secret—could make a difference in their relationship. He felt he had poured out his very soul to her. He told her everything about himself, still she had this secret. And why was she so afraid of sharing her secrets with him.

Finally, one day he kissed her goodbye early, telling her he had some chores to attend. Ellen started her walk home.

But John had another plan in mind. Whatever secret Ellen was hiding was clearly at her home. So he ducked into the weeds and hid behind trees until she was nearly out of sight, then he followed her along the railroad for over a mile.

Suddenly he lost sight of her. He knew she must have gone into one of three houses to the right of the roadway. The trouble was he wasn't sure which one. If he knocked at the wrong door, it could spoil everything. He decided to creep along the backyards to see if he found anything suspicious. And he did.

There behind the middle house, playing in the dirt was a small and neglected-looking child.

John called out and said, "Hello, son. What's your name?"

The boy said, "Tommy Hyden."

John didn't say anything more. He just walked away.

John began to avoid Ellen. She would ask when they would see each other again and he would make an excuse. Finally, she demanded to know what was happening.

"Tommy!" he told her bluntly. "Why didn't you tell me you had a child?"

Ellen stuttered and stammered but managed to say, "But I don't have a child. I mean, he's not mine—he's my brother."

"Then where's his parents?"

"I told you," she said. "My father's dead, and my mother ran off."

John said, "Well, it all might have been different if you had told me in the beginning."

Then Ellen got angry. "Do I need to remind you that *you* chased *me*? This is why I didn't want to get involved with you—or anyone, for that matter."

John just said, "Look, Ellen, I'm sorry. This is just a little too much for me. We've spent entire days together. We went away for three full days. Who was looking after that child all that time?"

Ellen was crushed. She knew it was over.

Two full days passed without John contacting her. She was losing her mind. How could he just lose all feelings for her? The hurt then became anger. She began to slander John's name in public.

A week passed, and she still hadn't heard from John. It was the last week in July 1913. She got up early and told little Tommy she was taking him to pick berries. She came home alone.

She then walked into the Collins and Mayo office, where she found John.

"John," she said, walking up to him, "I want you to know I sent Tommy away."

He eyed her carefully. "Where did you send Tommy?" His voice betrayed his doubt.

"I heard from my mother," she said. "So I sent Tommy to her on the train."

John quickly ushered Ellen out of the office, saying he would talk to her later about the matter. Without delay, he contacted C&O and asked if a small child had traveled alone on the train. They said no.

A search party was formed. After nine days, little Tommy was found. He had been decapitated.

Ellen Hyden was arrested before a mob could form. John Benson was cleared of any charges, but he had had enough. He abruptly quit Collins and Mayo and moved back to Pittsburgh.

The entire community attended little Tommy's burial. His body became the second to be buried on the Johnson family cemetery. The following year, the town's people purchased a marble headstone for him.

Chapter Twenty-Two

When Taube and Ida named their twins Joe and Floyd, it created some confusion. To alleviate the problem, the uncles simply became known as Old Joe and Old Floyd, and the nephews were Young Joe and Young Floyd.

It might be worth mentioning that the name Floyd was in honor of the frontiersman John Floyd. Floyd County was named for him as well. John Floyd was a friend and companion of the famous Daniel Boone. Originally from Virginia, Floyd hunted and trapped in Kentucky and convinced Boone to come to Kentucky.

Old Floyd Johnson met and married Lina Osborn. (No relation to Thomas Osborn, who was shot by Odell Geats.) They had their first child in late summer 1913. They named him Chris.

Floyd and Lina built a house on the mountaintop, not far from Floyd's sister, Dine, and her husband, Monk Hall. There were now four houses located along that ridge-line. They were three thousand feet up the path along the rocky gully Lische had named the Spring Fork. The front porches faced east, and the back porches faced west. The house to the north and east was a well-established farm that belonged to a man by the name of Bob Rogers.

These people lived on the mountaintop for the beauty. It was certainly not for the convenience. The closest modern amenities were miles away. Wells had to be dug deeper, firewood soon became scarce, and there was an almost-constant battle with snakes and wild animals, yet they remained. Even though there were hardships to endure, just living in this Garden of Eden made it all worthwhile. There couldn't have been a prettier place to live.

They were almost completely self-sufficient. They grew flowers and vegetable gardens. They planted apple, plum, cherry and peach trees. Each morning was a treat to watch the sun come up over the far distant mountains of West Virginia. It was an equal pleasure to watch the sun set in the west, then return to watch a full moon rising. But alas, all this beauty was almost erased by the high elevation winter winds.

Old Joe married a woman named Liza in 1915. When they were looking for their own place, he asked Lische for advice in selecting a site. He wanted something secluded. Lische had the perfect place in mind.

So Joe met up with his grandfather early on a Saturday morning. At almost seventy-three, Lische was showing very little signs of age. He walked or rode a horse for miles each day, he didn't overeat, and he never let anything worry him. He and Joe saddled up. Lische had a number of fine horses, and he seldom rode the same horse two days in a row. He had an uncanny way with them. He would select a horse according to the task or the trail. Today he would ride a four-year-old dark red gelding. He had ridden this horse before on mountain trails. Joe was only twenty-four-years old and less patient with animals. This was a trait inherited from his father. Coss had very little tolerance for a jumpy or unyielding horse.

Lische led the way as they rode up the trail along Spring Fork Creek. They stopped to chat briefly with Floyd and Lina as they passed their house. They rode to within sight of the Bob Rogers' place, then turned left and down the mountain. But the soft black dirt and the steep grade proved to be too awkward for the horses. They found an almost level patch of ground, tethered the horses, and continued on foot.

Not far from the top of the mountain, they broke into a clearing. There looked to be at least five acres of cleared land. The view of the valley below was stunning.

Joe turned to Lische and asked, "Who cleared this land?"

Lische said, "Mother Nature cleared it. A twister touched down here in the spring of 1868. It knocked all the trees down, then a brush fire did the rest. Come on—I'll show ya where to build your house."

They walked out onto a spot of ground that was almost level. There was a large boulder not much bigger than the average house. The front edge of the rock was about twenty feet high above the natural contour of the mountain. It had probably tumbled from the mountain above. Centuries of erosion had been dammed up behind it, creating a perfect place for a house. A small stream ran along the west side of the boulder that would provide cool, fresh water.

Joe couldn't believe his eyes. Lische watched and knew exactly what was going through his grandson's mind—he was building his farm in his mind. Lische knew because he had done the same, so many years ago.

Joe asked, "Do you know who owns this land?"

"Bob Rogers owns it, I think. And if he doesn't, then he'll know who does. Anyway, I'm sure you can get a good price on it, just cuz it's hard to get to. You said you wanted seclusion. Well, here it is. Now tell me what you plan to do here."

Well, obviously the house will be built here," Joe said. "I'll have to do some digging to level out a spot for the barn. But the rest will be filled with fruit trees."

Lische was almost as excited as his grandson. "Where do you plan to put your garden?"

Joe cleared his throat. "Well. . . uh. . . Grandpa, ya know I never cared too much for gardening."

"If you don't want to grow what you eat, then you'll have to have money to buy it," Lische said. "Therefore, you'll have to get a job. I never cared for being a slave in order to buy food, but I guess that's the way young folks do things today."

They sat for several hours planning and just gazing down into that beautiful green valley. There were no other houses to be seen; there was nothing but the birds and the animals.

Unlike his siblings, Joe didn't want a large family. He envisioned a small cottage with a front porch that extended right out to the edge of the boulder. This would give them an even loftier view of their valley. He would have morning glories enclosing the porch railing. All the windows would have flower boxes, where they would plant marigolds and asters. In the yard, there would be a windmill with hollyhocks growing beneath it.

But then Joe became beside himself. "What if Bob, or whoever the owner is, won't sell this land?"

"Oh, he'll sell all right. We'll put your father on it, and he'll get it done. I do have some advice for you, however: just buy yourself eighty acres. Don't buy this entire valley. You don't need it. It might be fifty years before anyone moves into this valley. When they do, they'll want to be all the way on the other end. That'll put them a little closer to Virgie or Pikeville."

Joe said, "That sounds like good advice, Grandpa."

Reluctantly, Coss brokered a deal with Bob Rogers for the eighty acres. Coss did not support his children in their decision to live in such seclusion. Floyd, Dine, and now Joe all lived up that mountain. Were his children crazy? Why on earth would anyone want to live in a wilderness after we worked so hard to bring in civilization?

Lische, on the other hand, understood completely. Furthermore, he was excited to get started. He took an ax and started clearing a trail down the mountain and through the valley. Joe would need supplies and building material and it would be easier to bring them from the Pike County side.

They built the house and did the landscaping right out of their imagination. In just a few short years, the fruit trees were growing and the flowers were blooming. Not once did Joe ever regret building his house in that location and he owed it all to his grandfather.

Floyd and Lina loved their mountaintop home as well. On Taube's thirtieth birthday, November 29, 1915, they had another son. They named him Hazadore. Coss continued to urge them to move back down into town, but they wouldn't hear of it.

Taube and Ida had another son in 1917. His name was Johnny.

That same year, the United States entered the Great War. For the most part, the area was unaffected. A few men volunteered, but with coal being such a vital component of the war, men working the industry were not taken to fight.

Chapter Twenty-Three

The years came and went. Taube continued his career in the machine shop, and they still ran the service station as well. There were more cars in the area, and he had to hire more help at the service station. Taube installed a train whistle on the roof of the machine shop. The whistle would sound to begin and end the work shift. The whistle would also sound in the event of an emergency.

Taube's brothers had helped build the railroad, but that work was now completed. They now rode great distances on horseback to work in the coal mines.

There was a mine opening not more than a hundred feet from the southeast corner of the machine shop. The mine ran approximately three hundred yards south under the mountain. One hundred yards to the west of that opening, another shaft was tunneled. This tunnel ran at an angle to connect with the existing mine. From that point, the main tunnel continued, splitting several times and stretching for miles under the mountain. A large electric fan was installed at the entrance of the second tunnel. It ran twenty-four hours a day to blow in fresh air.

On a summer morning in 1926, men came rushing from the mine entrance. There had been some kind of accident. They reported to Taube that a single boulder had dropped from the mine roof, and they thought a man was trapped under it.

Everyone was accounted for except for a man by the name of Buddy Ed Rice. They did not want to sound the alarm and announce the emergency until they were sure Buddy had come to work. Taube checked the time cards and found that Buddy had indeed reported for work. And then just to be sure Buddy had not left work early, Taube sent a man to the Rice home. The man came back at a hard gallop. Buddy was not at home. The rider had been careful not to alarm Buddy's wife.

Taube followed the crew back into the mine to assess the damage. The boulder was approximately twelve feet long, eight feet wide, and four feet thick. It would take a skilled blasting crew to break the boulder apart and find out if anyone had been trapped.

Late that evening, there was a long continuous blast of the whistle from the machine shop. People came from all over what is now called the Coal Camp to see what the emergency was. Everyone was frightened; they didn't yet know what had happened. Taube quietly gave instructions for a rider to carry the message back to the Rice family.

The rescue team recovered the body of twenty-four-year-old Buddy Ed Rice. The remains were so mangled; they had to be brought out in a box. Buddy had had a metal can of Prince Albert smoking tobacco in his hip pocket. The can was smashed completely flat.

Buddy was survived by his twenty-two-year-old wife, Eveline, and two children—a two-year-old daughter and a four-year-old son. Buddy also had a brother, Elliott, who was a coal miner as well.

The community shared the grief with total compassion. They knew the same such fate could come to their door. People were especially kind to Eveline and her two small children, now fatherless. They donated food and clothing and passed the collection plate for her at church.

But all the kindness of the world is sometimes not enough when fate comes calling. Seven months after Buddy's death, Eveline developed a cough, then a fever. No one knew how sick she was, and they certainly didn't know she had influenza. Eveline died in January 1927. Her daughter and son were orphaned.

Buddy's story would prove that mining coal was a dangerous business, but it was a way of life for many people in the area. Coal companies sought men with experience, but they would hire anyone willing and able to do the work. No specific level of education was required, only a willingness to go underground. Men came from all over the country to work the coal. Some were criminals or bandits. Others came from great distances to reinvent themselves. They could (if they wanted to) make a brand new start.

Some workers were fortunate enough to have jobs on the surface. Conveyer belts were sometimes used to carry coal from the mine shafts to what was called a tipple. A tipple was used to store the coal until it was picked up by the train or trucks; much like a farmer uses a silo. Men would stand alongside the conveyer belt and sort out any impurities, such rock or slate. Those men were envied and sometimes despised for not having to go underground.

The brakemen also worked on the surface, but they had a much more dangerous job. They had to work with the coal guns. Men would often underestimate the steepness of the railroad, resulting in tragedy. Arms and legs were lost. Frank Johnson lost an arm, and just two years later E. C. Johnson (no relation to Frank) lost his arm as well.

Sometimes brakemen were crushed. Such was the case with Orville Olney. He thought he had secured the brake, but it was not quite enough to keep the coal gun from rolling. He was between the cars with his back turned when he was pinned. Lucky for him, it happened during shift change, so a large group of men were nearby. Twenty or so men were able to separate the cars enough to free Orville. He survived, but he had a long and painful recovery.

There was plenty of danger in the coal industry. However, deaths and injuries were relatively few, especially when you consider the number of men who went under the mountain each day and the millions of tons extracted. In fact, more people were killed in shootouts or knife fights.

To tell the truth, sometimes life in general is hazardous. For instance, sometimes accidents or incidents occurred through nothing less than stupidity or alcohol-induced stupor.

Such was the case with Dine's husband, Monk. Walking home one winter night, he decided there was enough moonshine liquor in him to keep him from freezing. So he stopped for a nap along the trail. By sheer coincidence, two men happened along the trail and found Monk frozen to the ground. Monk survived, but frostbite on his backside and the infection that followed nearly cost him his life.

Willie Cole also fell under the influence of moonshine, but he wouldn't be so lucky. He drank enough moonshine to believe he could knock the train from its track. The incident took place in Melvin in 1928.

Most people had become complacent to the sound of the afternoon train whistle. Willie, however, told everyone how much he hated that damned noisy old train. No one thought he was serious when he would say, 'I'm going to knock that old Mellie engine right off the track.'

And then one day, the train came in with the engineer blowing a constant whistle. With the moonshine urging him on, this was the day Willie would finally do it.

There were a number of witnesses, but no one was close enough to stop him. Onlookers could only stare with disbelief as Willie met the speeding train at a dead run. The train struck Willie, then dragged him several hundred yards along the tracks before it came to a stop. It was a grisly scene. The train had to back up in order to retrieve bits and pieces of Willie's remains.

In the summer of 1929, five teenaged boys discovered how dangerous life could suddenly be, even without alcohol. The boys were romping around atop Collier Rock one afternoon. It was Old Floyd's two sons, Chris and Hazadore, Taube's twins, Young Joe and Young Floyd; and Abe Hampton.

The boys sat down to rest near a large oak standing about ten feet from the edge of the cliff. No one is certain just how high the cliff is at that point, but let's just say it's a dizzying height. The tree grew at about a thirty-five-degree angle over the edge of the cliff. A large grapevine about two inches in diameter ran on the top side of the tree trunk, extending and branching into the treetop.

Thirteen-year-old Abe casually reclined himself against the tree trunk. As the boys talked, he nonchalantly carved at the grapevine under his leg, with a pocket knife. But the moment he carved through the vine, the weight of the vine retracted back, taking Abe with it. The boy instinctively grabbed the vine and swung out over the cliff. Like a scene from a Tarzan movie, the boy went on a long and terrifying swing twenty stories above the forest below. He dangled at least fifty feet below the tree, at the end of the vine.

Abe began to scream and pray. The other boys were screaming as well, all of them trying to tell Abe what to do. Abe knew that dropping was not an option. And he wouldn't be able to swing the vine back to the cliff. He had only one chance for survival. He had to climb the vine into the tree, and then climb down the tree to safety.

The boy screamed, "I can't look up or down!"

Chris yelled back, "Don't do either! Just climb!"

Fortunately, Abe was skinny enough, strong enough, and full of enough adrenaline to start climbing. The terrified boys watched as he inched his way upward. They all knew that one slip, one mistake, or one weak muscle would send the boy to certain death on the rocks below.

The tense moments were like hours, but Abe finally made it to the treetop. While the trunk of the tree was angled, its branches grew straight up to catch the sun. Therefore, Abe would have to pass each branch on one side or the other.

He nervously clutched the branches with a death grip. Small twigs and pieces of bark dropped to the forest below. At last he made it out of the branches to the trunk of the tree.

This should have been the easy part of the ordeal, but the exhausted boy couldn't reach around the trunk. Chris instructed him to lie on his stomach, keep himself balanced, hold tight to the bark, and slide himself down, butt first.

Finally, after more than an hour, Abe was safe. The other boys had to pry his hands loose from the tree. They carried him far from the edge of the cliff and placed him in a soft bed of moss. He rested there for more than two hours. Even then, he was still unable to walk. The other boys took turns carrying him down the mountain.

They stopped to rest along the way, reflecting on the event. Joe, Floyd, and Hazadore began to giggle at first. Then they laughed heartily.

Joe said, "Did you see the look on his face when he went over that cliff?"

"Yeah, it was hilarious!" Floyd said.

Chris spoke up and said, "I didn't see anything funny. What I saw was death."

Chapter Twenty-Four

Coal is found in layers called seams. If a coal seam is discovered to be thirty-two inches in height, it will very likely remain at or close to that height. Even if the seam runs for miles, its thickness rarely changes.

Early in the twentieth century, the large companies had a heyday when they first opened mines in eastern Kentucky. They first found and mined the tall, easy-to-reach coal. They didn't bother with anything shorter than a forty-two-inch seam. However, as the years passed, they either settled for smaller coal seams or they packed up and moved on.

Whenever a large company pulled out, several smaller ones took its place. The demand for coal was still increasing, even as more and more homeowners turned to natural gas or electricity for heat and lighting. In fact, as the demand for steel and electricity increased, so did coal production. In large industrial cities, smoke from power plants and blast furnaces billowed into the air around the clock, seven days a week.

But the Roaring Twenties were coming to an end. There was change in the air, but most people were oblivious to it.

Industry had been booming for more than three decades. However, Lische had always warned his family not to have all their investments in one place. He had also warned them of the risk in paper money.

Taube and Ida had their final child in 1929. They named him Charles. Little did they know what was in store for their young family.

On the thirtieth day of October 1929, the morning train brought word that the banks had failed. The news was slow to sink in with the masses. What did it mean? So what if the stock market crashed? They still had their money.

It took a long time for people to realize their money had no value. Then the questions were endless. Yes, they still had their jobs, but how could they keep going to work if they couldn't be paid? What about the power plants? How could they operate if people can't afford to pay their bills? Why deliver food to the markets if no one can buy it?

Lische was now eighty-nine years old, but he still had a youthful wit. Coss was seventy, and Taube was about to turn forty-five. Taube was a little concerned, but he knew his father and grandfather would have some answers. Everyone knew it was time for a family meeting. Coss would host the meeting at his place.

The weather was unseasonably warm and dry, so they had an early dinner in the yard. Counting the wives and grandchildren, Lische's family had now grown to twenty-one. Coss had a long picnic table in the shade of a large beech tree for just such occasions.

After dinner, the children were told to go somewhere to play—and to do it quietly. Coss then opened a bottle of brandy and passed out cigars. Joe and Floyd declined. Both men were obviously troubled, for they had not invested well.

All were silent until Floyd spoke first. "Well, I think this whole thing's going to blow over."

"Yeah, me too," Joe said. "I mean, how can everything suddenly be worthless?"

Taube nodded, and then said, "I haven't seen anything change so far. Men are still going to work. The trains are still running. I think it will have to blow over."

Lische was holding a Sears and Roebuck catalog. He asked, "How much cash do you three have in paper form?"

The three men looked at each other, at their father, and then at their grandfather. Floyd said, "Well, sir, quite a bit."

Lische took some pages from the catalog and ripped them to pieces. "This is what your paper money is now worth," he said as he dropped it to the ground.

Knowing his two brothers were ashamed to voice the obvious question, Taube had to be the one to ask, "So what should we do?"

"We're not going to do anything," Coss said. "I learned to take my father's advice many years ago. Our bank will fail, just like the rest of them. But that's why we brought in partners. If we hadn't, we would be in the same sinking ship with the rest of the country. Also, it's a good thing we have our family's cash reserves neither in a bank nor in paper form. Our reserves are in the form of twenty-dollar gold piece."

"How much do we have in gold, Father?" Joe asked.

"That's not for you to know at this time, because we're not going to spend a penny of it," Coss replied.

Then Lische said, "I'm gonna give you boys some advice. No, let me rephrase that. I'm gonna give you some *orders*, and you better follow them closely if you know what's good for you. We have plenty of food for the winter, but when spring comes, it's time for you to go to work. You're going to plant gardens. You're going to grow every kind of vegetable you can think of. You're going to clear new ground, and you're going to plant corn and green beans. You're going to tend to your fruit trees and your livestock. You're going to pick every berry that ripens on the vine. It's still going to be tough, but if you do all that, we'll make it."

"And I'm going to add a little more to what he just said," Coss stated. "If you have money that's worth anything, hang on to it. Don't be seen in public with money. People will become desperate. A man never knows what he'll do until his children begin to starve. First they'll try to borrow, then they'll beg, then they'll steal, and then they'll rob. If you need something, trade something for it, work for it, or barter for it. Remember to hang on to your work animals and your tools. Guard them closely. Folks will be after them as well."

Chapter Twenty-Five

By the mid-1930s, Floyd and Lina had a large family. When they were through, they would have ten children, including a set of twins. Floyd worked in a coal mine, and Lina took care of the children. They soon realized they could no longer live on the mountaintop. No one had lived in Lische's old cabin for some time, but it was still sturdy and dry. With a little cleaning and fixing up, they were able to move into it.

Dine and Monk remained on the mountaintop. The view alone was an equal trade-off to the harsh conditions.

They had lost their first two children at birth and were afraid to try again. But as the biological clock ticked and other people's children played around them, they decided to try again. This time their baby lived. Charley was born in 1932. He would be their only child, but he would have lots of cousins to grow up with.

Monk was hoeing corn on a late spring day in 1934. The weather had been unusually hot and dry. The cornfield was about a hundred yards from the house just below the crest of the hill on the east side of the mountain. Monk was getting thirsty. It was nearly midday. Just a few more strokes of the hoe, and he would walk home for a lunch break.

Monk left his hoe in place and started for home. He had only taken a few steps when he heard a strange sound. He froze in place, trying to figure out what he had heard. Then he could make out the growling and snarling of dogs fighting not too far away. He looked around and noticed his dog was no longer resting in the shade of the apple tree. Monk turned back, grabbed the hoe, and ran to save his dog. Just then, he saw his dog streaking past in the trail above the field. He was running for his life.

Soon after, a large brown dog followed. He almost looked harmless at first. He wasn't actually chasing Monk's dog. But as Monk got closer to the trail, he could see the dog's mouth was bloody and he was covered in mud. From the low growl, Monk knew the dog was rabid.

Monk raced after the dog, yelling and waving his arms to draw his attention, but to no avail. The dog was headed straight for Monk's home, where his unsuspecting wife and child were enjoying a routine day. Monk raced after him.

Monk knew Dine had the doors and windows open, taking advantage of the mountain breeze. He began screaming for his wife to close and lock the doors. Just as the mad dog approached the house, Monk saw the back door shut. Long seconds passed, and then the front door closed. Monk could no longer see the dog. There could only be one answer: the dog had jumped through the back window.

Monk hit the back door at a dead run, knocking it open and falling to the kitchen floor. Stunned and confused, the dog was standing completely still not six feet from Monk's terrified wife and child.

In a single motion, Monk leaped forward and struck the dog with the hoe. The dog fell on his side, then scrambled to its feet and charged. Monk punched him squarely on the nose. The blow only knocked the dog back a few feet but he charged again. It became clear that the dog was completely impervious to pain. He just kept attacking.

Dine and little Charley were screaming in horror as Monk fought for his life. Monk was screaming for Dine to open the front door, then dash into the side room. With Charley on her hip, she fumbled with the door lock as the battle continued. At last, the door opened and Dine ducked out of sight.

Monk continued punching the dog, pushing him back, sometimes a few feet and sometimes only a few inches. The dog caught the hoe handle in his mouth, shaking it violently. Monk twisted it free and punched again. Finally, Monk pushed the dog out onto the front porch. Monk took one more desperate swing, knocking the dog to the side. The animal suddenly froze in place for a moment, then simply got up and walked away. Monk watched in disbelief as the dog disappeared on the trail leading toward Bob Rogers' place.

Knowing that Bob's wife was likely to be home alone, Monk raced into the house for his shotgun. He told Dine to lock herself and Charley in the bedroom and not make a sound. He then set out after the dog.

He found the dog not more than a hundred yards down the trail. The dog was dead, whether from the blows Monk had inflicted or from the disease.

Monk wasted no time. He buried the dog before other animals could come. Otherwise, they would be infected as well. He made a large rock pile over the grave to keep scavengers from digging into the remains.

Back home, there was not a moment to lose. The entire house had to be disinfected. Any bodily fluids, especially saliva, from a rabid animal are as contagious as the common cold. The walls, the floor, and anything the dog might have touched had to be scrubbed with lye soap and water. Luckily, the mad dog hadn't gone near the barn or the livestock.

An infected animal can go for days, even weeks, without showing symptoms. A rabid animal is like a time bomb, and nature sets the trigger. When the disease at last becomes obvious, nothing can be done.

So Monk knew there would be one more dog to bury. Their faithful hunting dog and beloved family pet was surely infected from his fight with the mad dog. He would have to be destroyed. Monk put a leash on the obedient old dog and led him away from the house.

Charley watched from the window, curiously wondering why his dog was being taken away. Sensing something was wrong, the child began to wail. Dine told Monk to bring the dog back and tie him to a tree in the yard until nightfall, when Charley would be asleep. That night in the pale half-moon light, Monk led the humble old dog down an eerie trail to his death.

The next day was a God sent act of mercy. About mid-morning, thunderstorms formed in the southwestern sky. For almost an hour, sheets of rain swept across the mountaintops. Nature was washing away the mad dog's infected blood and saliva. But how many animals had the dog bitten? And how had the dog been infected to begin with?

Word of the mad dog spread quickly. Not long after, Bob Rogers quit the mountain and moved his family to Pikeville. Joe and Liza were a bit farther down the mountain, but no one was left on the mountaintop now except Monk, Dine, and little Charley.

They felt completely alone, much the way a child feels when his classmates run away and leave him behind. This was such a beautiful life, but it could also be tragic.

Oddly enough, it was Dine who wanted to remain. She remembered what her grandfather had always said: 'There are some years when nothing works the way it should. Those years will come, and they will pass.'

Monk was easily convinced. He loved living there as well. But in the first week of August, they would be tested again.

Chapter Twenty-Six

It was Sunday afternoon. The day had been extremely hot. It was the time of the year when the birds had hatched their second brood and didn't have much to sing about. The chickens had gathered in the shade of the barn, and they too were quieter than usual. The only sound on this lazy afternoon was the occasional clunking of the cowbell.

It was mid-afternoon and the sun was no longer directly overhead, the front porch facing east presented a cool shade for Monk and Dine. They relaxed on the porch reading while little Charley played with small toys in the yard.

About four p.m., they heard a low rumble, which they thought was distant blasting; A short while later, they heard the sound again. This time, it sounded a little different than before.

"That might be thunder," Monk said. He then pointed to a large poplar tree. "I'm sure it's thunder—look at those leaves."

The poplar's leaves had turned, revealing the lighter-green bottom side. According to the old folks, this was an absolute promise of rain.

Dine and Monk gathered Charley and walked through the house to the back porch for another view. They were elated to see a storm forming miles away to the southwest. They needed the rain, and perhaps the storm would offer some relief from the heat.

It was fascinating as they watched how incredibly fast the storm was forming. The clouds appeared to stretch from the mountaintops to the floor of the heavens. The clouds rolled, swelled, and multiplied. There were spectacular colors: shades of blue, gray, white, and sea green. Lightning flashed, and a short time later, a low rumble of thunder could be heard. As the storm grew closer, the thunder and lightning became more frequent.

Monk and Dine noticed that the family's horse, mule, milk cow, hogs, and chickens had all moved into the barn. Nature has its way of protecting itself when storms become ominous. This was a warning that the storm would probably be more than just a summer shower.

For a moment, the storm was almost silent and an almost cold breeze blew across the mountains. The leading edge of the cloud was right over the house, when seconds later, the first hailstones bounced on the dusty ground.

Then the storm took on a strange sound. It wasn't the sound of thunder or wind, but a sound much like the waves on an angry sea. The distant mountains had vanished as if they were never there. Soon the ground became white with walnut-sized hail.

The family hurried inside and closed the doors and windows. The sound of the hail on the roof was deafening, but Monk assured Dine that the thick wooden shingles would protect them.

After about twenty minutes, the storm was much quieter. It was not much more than a heavy downpour now. Monk and Dine ventured back to the porch. They were astonished at what the hail had left behind. The yard was completely covered with leaves. The storm had all but stripped the trees bare.

The rain continued until just after dark. Then the sky cleared, and the temperature and the humidity dropped to a chill. About ten p.m., a slightly waning full moon appeared above the mountains. The moonlight glistened on the wet leaves that now covered the ground. The night sky had never been more beautiful. All was quiet, and the cool night should have been a pleasant one for sleeping. But there would be no sleep and no conversation. They knew the hail had stripped more than just leaves from the trees.

The next morning, they went out to assess the damage. They were saddened but not surprised to find the fruit trees and the gardens decimated. If they were lucky enough to have a late winter—sometime around Christmas—they might have time to find a way to survive. In the back of his mind, Monk thought of asking his miserly old father-in-law Coss for a handout, but he dismissed the notion. They knew it would be tough, but they were sure they would make it.

Monk left on foot, heading for Joe and Liza's place to see how they had weathered the storm. The path from the top of the mountain down to Joe's cabin was too steep for a horse. And with the way things were, the last thing Monk needed was a lame horse.

Monk found Joe on the front porch. Monk didn't have to ask; the damage was obvious.

Monk told Joe of his plan to head to Virgie, roughly ten miles away. There were a number of coal mines along the route. Maybe one of them would be interested in purchasing timbers or would otherwise have work to offer. If he didn't find work by Virgie, he would continue to Pikeville or Whitesburg.

Joe said he'd join him, so they saddled up and rode together. They tried to remain optimistic, but in the days of the Depression, men stood in line just to beg.

It was late afternoon, and neither man had eaten. So far, they'd been turned down at every mine. It was hard to be optimistic on an empty stomach, but they pressed on. A few of the mines they passed seemed to have been recently abandoned. Others had handwritten signs that read, "We're not hiring, so please don't ask."

They came to a mine about two miles from Virgie, they were encouraged to see seven loaded coal guns and an eighth below the tipple being loaded with coal. The mine was owned by Inland Steel. They caught the foreman in the nick of time. His day was over, and he was walking to his truck. They hated to delay the man from going home after a hard day, but they were desperate.

Joe was a little older and a lot more outgoing, so he rode right up and asked, "Mister, could you use a couple hundred timbers for this operation?"

They just couldn't believe it when the man said, "Actually, I could use five hundred at this site and another six hundred at my Elkhorn City location. My name is Lloyd Hall. Who do I have the pleasure of meeting?"

"My name is Joe Johnson, and this is Monk Hall," Joe said.

"Hall, huh? We might be related, although Halls and Johnsons are thicker than weeds in these parts. Well, gentlemen, what I need here is five hundred at forty-four inches in length. They have to be at least five inches in diameter at the tip. If they aren't, I'll cull them and I will not pay you for them. The same rule applies to the six hundred for Elkhorn. The length on those is thirty-eight inches. I prefer hardwood, but I'll accept poplar if they're straight. I'll pay you five cents each if you have the means to deliver them—but seeing as you're on horseback, I assume you don't."

For a moment, their hearts sank; they thought the deal was off.

But then Lloyd said, "I can send a coal truck for them if you can get them to a place where we can reach them. But then the price becomes four cents apiece."

"Lloyd, you don't know how much we appreciate this," Joe said. "We passed a number of mines that were shut down, yet your company looks to be booming. We thought the steel mills were shut down like the rest of the factories. Can I ask what your secret is?"

"Well, it's true that we're not producing a lot of steel. But we have a contract with the Tennessee Valley Power Authority. They're generating massive amounts of electricity. They're buying every ton of coal we can send them. They're getting government money, you see." Lloyd paused and looked at the two men. "Not that I'm taking on employees, but I was surprised when you didn't ask for jobs."

"We're usually self-sufficient," Joe replied, "but the hailstorm on Sunday wiped out this year's crop."

"Hailstorm? You must live high on the hill."

Joe said, "I live near the top, and Monk lives on the top."

"Are you boys related?" Lloyd asked.

"Yes sir, Monk is married to my sister."

"Well, I'm looking forward to doing business with you boys. But if you tell a single soul about this, the deal is off." Lloyd lowered his voice. "I don't want a long line of hungry men standing here when I come to work tomorrow. I've had to turn away so many hungry men—and I know they have hungry wives and children as well. A man should never be in a position to beg in this country, and a man should never be in a position to refuse someone who begs. I swear to you, sometimes I wish I could trade places with the men I have to turn away."

Joe and Monk headed back home with the good news about their deal with Lloyd. They got started cutting timber while Liza and Dine salvaged what they could from the fruit trees and the gardens. It appeared everything would work out after all. The whole scenario must have been divine intervention. The hailstorm had obviously been an act of nature, but finding work was nothing short of a miracle.

They supplied Lloyd the eleven hundred timbers, but then the orders kept coming. Lloyd Hall had saved them.

Winter set in just after Thanksgiving. Soon the snow was just too deep to continue logging. They had enough food to keep them from starving during the winter, but certain items began to run out in February. They needed flour, cornmeal, and sugar. And although it was a luxury, they could sure use some coffee. They had used the same coffee grounds until it hardly colored the water.

Somehow Monk had to make it to the store. Wheelwright had a better selection of goods, but Virgie was closer. Besides, Joe and Liza were probably in the same boat, and they were closer to Virgie.

It was clear and very cold when Monk set out on his journey to Virgie at only the slightest hint of dawn. Like most men of that time and that area, Monk was accustomed to hard labor. But this would prove to be the most exhausting day he had ever had to endure.

The snow was just over a foot deep, but there had been enough of a January thaw and refreeze to create a thin crust of ice on top. The ice was almost thick enough to hold his weight, but not quite. If he'd had snowshoes, it would have been much easier. As it was, he could walk on top of the snow for a few steps, and then it would break through. Sometimes he would only stumble, and sometimes he would fall, yet he never once thought of turning back.

He was already worn out when he reached Joe and Liza's cabin about ten a.m. They too were running out of supplies, but they were a little better off than Monk and Dine. Even so, Joe was more than willing to ride to Virgie with Monk.

The journey was slow. Even in the cold, the horses were sweating. But Monk knew he had to make this trip to Virgie and back—and he had to make it before dark. Ever since the mad dog incident, Dine was terrified of being home alone, especially at night.

Finally, Monk looked at his brother-in-law. "Joe, this is the last straw. I'm going to move my family off that mountain, and I'm going to do it soon."

"Well, I can't say that I blame you," Joe said. "You can build a house right next to our place, if you want."

"You know, I don't even want to live that high on the mountain."

"In that case," Joe said, "I've got the perfect place in mind. I'll show it to you on the way back.

Joe knew of some bottom-land just high enough above the creek to be safe from flash flooding. There was ample space for a small farm. The reposing sound of Indian Creek was enough of a trade-off for the mountaintop view Monk and Dine were giving up. It was there that Monk built the house they would live in for the rest of their lives.

Chapter Twenty-Seven

As the long years of the Depression dragged on the people suffered, they starved and many of them died. Frankie was not a victim of the depression, but she passed away in 1936. Coss just immersed himself in his work, as his father had done when his mother had passed away. When there was nothing to do, Coss would start some new project—anything to pass the time.

Lische, now well into his nineties, was no longer the clean-cut and upright figure of a man he had once been. He no longer attempted to shave or get a haircut. He never stopped roaming the mountains and said he hoped to die there. Young boys told fearful stories of a wild mountain man who roamed the woods.

The Depression was at least as tough as Lische and Coss had warned. Desperate people attempted to grow food on land that was completely untillable. They dug up their yards and their walkways, yet they starved. Everyone blamed it all on President Hoover. Wise men knew, however, that the true cause was the greed that lies dormant in the belly of every human being until money makes it grow.

Many young men became tired of working in vain, so they joined the military with the hope of being fed. In the summer of 1938, Taube's twenty-one-year old son, Johnny, joined the Marines, maybe or maybe not for that same reason. Just over a year later, Hitler's Germany invaded Poland.

Needless to say, business had been slow for Taube and Ida through the 1930s. They didn't let it bother them; they just kept working and saving money here and there. They were doing well compared to friends and relatives with financial woes. They felt little sense of chivalry for those who were unprepared for troubled times. Sure, they felt sorry for their friends and neighbors, but those problems were too big for them to remedy. If they had embraced the wisdom of their elders, they would have been much better off.

In 1940, Taube purchased a few acres of land in Weeksbury, complete with the mineral rights. He hired some excavators, and found a thirty-six-inch coal seam. Within six months, the mine was producing two hundred tons of coal per week. By the fall of 1941, he owned three mines and his wealth continued to grow.

Taube and Ida's youngest son, Charles, was now twelve years old. This gave Ida more freedom to pursue her small business interests. They built a new home midway between Weeksbury and Wheelwright. They also built a barn and fences, then bought and traded fine horses. They owned two vehicles.

Taube asked his father if he wanted a car or truck, but Coss responded, "Not until they stop making horses."

We all know what happened on December 7, 1941. But for anyone who had a loved one in the military at the time, the Pearl Harbor attack was even more troubling. Ida was up late every night, reading books or walking the floor. They hadn't heard from Johnny for some time and she always feared the worst.

As the winter and spring of 1942 passed with very little military response from the United States, Ida's mind became more at ease. Although there had been some fighting in such places as Wake Island and Corregidor, there had been no major offensive against the Japanese. Ida knew Johnny was stationed with the First Marine Division, and they had not yet deployed. Or at least she thought they hadn't deployed. In mid-June, word came of the naval victory near the Midway Islands.

In early July, they received a letter from Johnny. He was alive and doing well in New Zealand. The Midway battle had been fought between ships and planes and as he was an infantryman and he was unaffected. He went on to say that his division was training hard for something. He had no idea what, but they would soon find out.

As it turned out, they were training for an immediate invasion of the island of Guadalcanal. The Japanese empire was scattered throughout the Pacific. Guadalcanal lies just north of the Coral Sea. It is the largest and southernmost island of the Solomon Island chain. For more than two decades, the Japanese had worked to fortify the island. What troubled American commanders most was reconnaissance photos showing that a long strip of jungle had been cut away. The Japanese were building a runway.

Major General Alexander Vandergrift led the First Marine Division. He warned Washington that he needed more time to prepare for such a large-scale operation. He took his concerns to Admirals Halsey and Nimitz. They explained the three main reasons why the invasion needed to be immediate. First and foremost, they needed to stop the completion of the Japanese airfield. Second, they needed the element of surprise. The Japanese were not expecting a major offensive from the United States until sometime in 1943. And the third reason was the American people were tired of having their asses handed to them. It was time to make the other fellow bleed. The admirals told Vandergrift he would have until the first week in August to prepare.

In the early hours of August 7, 1942—eight months to the day after the Pearl Harbor attack—it began. All the fury of hell was unleashed on Guadalcanal. After hours of relentless bombardment, the First Marine Division went ashore under heavy fire. Johnny was now in combat.

As news came in of the invasion, Taube tried to console his wife. He told her it was all in the hands of God; mortal men could do little to change what was to come. But nothing could stop Ida from worrying about Johnny. She had heard of the atrocities of war, and she imagined her son having to endure every one of them.

The next letter they received from Johnny was in early November. He only told them he was on Guadalcanal. He was careful not to use words such as *combat* or *fighting*. He only asked his parents not to worry.

Long, weary days of the war dragged on. On the home front, mornings were spent reading every word written about the latest developments of the war. Evenings were spent huddled around the radio. The Battle for Guadalcanal lasted until February 1943, when the Marines at last captured the airfield. A sign at the end of the runway had read: 'Hirohito's Air Base'. The Marines replaced it with a new sign: 'Under New Management'. The airstrip was later named Henderson Field, in honor of Major Lofton Henderson, a Marine pilot who was shot down over Midway.

Johnny had been there through the entire battle. He was proud of their first victory. But it was only the beginning. Johnny fought in one campaign after another throughout island chains such as the Solomon Islands, the Mariana Islands, the Marshall Islands, and the Philippines. There were battle names such as Tarawa, Tinian, Betio, Peleliu, and Saipan.

Then in June 1943, Johnny was in a transport plane going from Mindanao to Henderson Field. The plane was struck by flak from anti-aircraft fire. The plane was going down fast. Within minutes, the men were scrambling for the door. They bailed out over the small island of Rendova. The plane was at such a low altitude when Johnny jumped, his parachute didn't deploy in time to slow his descent. He landed in a tree, breaking his left leg. Agents of the Coast Watchers military intelligence organisation saw the plane go down and radioed for help. Six months later, Johnny's leg was healed, and he was back in action.

On September 15, 1944, as Johnny and the First Marine Division were preparing for an amphibious assault on Saipan there was a sad day back home. It would take months for Johnny to learn that on that very day, the Johnson family patriarch had died peacefully in his sleep.

Lische passed away one day before his 104th birthday. He had lived to see four generations after him. By the early 1940s, Old Floyd's two eldest sons, Chris and Hazadore, had married and had children of their own.

Lische's family had known his days were drawing to a close. In the end, he was a mere shadow of his former self. He no longer held the wisdom or practiced the wholesome habits that had made him a tower of a man for so many years. He had continued his daily strolls, but he sometimes lost his way. Coss or Taube would have to find him and escort him home. He sometimes called people by the wrong name or forgot who they were all together. The extensive knowledge he once had of the trees, plants, and animals had faded away.

As odd as it might seem, Coss wouldn't allow his father to be buried next to Sally. He knew Lische had never been able to bear the thought of Sally's grave. He could never stand to even visit it. Therefore, Coss had Lische buried near the cabin where he had spent the last thirty-nine years of his life.

Chapter Twenty-Eight

Without a doubt, the most fortified place in the Pacific was the volcanic sand and ash covered island of Iwo Jima. In February 1945, navy guns opened up as Marine and navy dive bombers pounded the island. So much fire and destruction blasted the island that the Marines thought they would have an easy victory. They were wrong. The Japanese were well positioned and dug in within concrete bunkers known as pillboxes, therefore the heavy bombardment was almost ineffective. The Japanese forces were commanded by the most brilliant man in the Japanese land forces, General Kuribayashi.

The navy bombardment ceased, and the Marines landed on the southeast end of the island under heavy fire. Their first objective was a tall volcanic mound called Mount Suribachi. Within hours, they had taken the mountain and raised the American flag.

Later that day, Joseph Rosenthal took his famous photo. He wanted to photograph the original group who had raised the flag earlier. However, one of the men had already been wounded, and one had been killed.

The Marines then turned northeast to capture one of three airfields located on the island. The Battle of Iwo Jima lasted just over three weeks. The US commanders declared victory in mid-March 1945.

Okinawa was the next hurdle for the Marines. That battle was launched on the first day of April 1945. After the victory at Okinawa, the United States and the Allies had an airfield within striking distance of the Japanese mainland.

Back home, Johnny's brother, Joe, had been drafted into the US Army Air Corps. He was sent to Okinawa, where he would load ordnance onto long-range bombers headed for Japanese cities. Louis Fieser, a chemist at Harvard University, had developed a new weapon. It was a gasoline-based gelatin known as napalm. Napalm had been used to incinerate cities in Germany. The temperature in the streets of Dresden was said to have reached one thousand degrees. Now this hellish fury was being used to burn large cities on the Japanese mainland to ash. Still, Japan refused to surrender.

Hitler was now dead and there was peace in Europe, and now all eyes were on the Japanese mainland. The United States and the Allies were preparing for an all-out invasion. It was said that a million men would be needed.

Ida hadn't said too much about it, but the war was taking its toll on her. She worked hard and kept herself busy, but she now had two sons in harm's way. Millions had died all over the world since the war started. She kept asking herself how long her sons would be exempt from death.

We all know what happened next. The A-bomb was dropped, the war ended. Johnny and Joe would soon be on their way home.

Johnny never left the Marine Corps. There was something about it that he loved. Joe was honorably discharged from the service. He took a job at Island Creek Coal Company and bought a small house near Melvin.

Joe started dating a lady by the name of Fannie Cole, who was twelve years his senior. Fannie was the granddaughter of Willie Cole, who tried to knock the train off the tracks. Joe and Fannie's relationship was tumultuous from the beginning. Fannie was an attractive lady. Throughout her entire life, she looked and acted like a 1940s movie star. She always dressed the part, complete with the horn-rimmed glasses. She was somewhat quiet in nature, until she became cross—she then had the temper of a polecat.

Joe was also a man of the forties. He was always well-dressed and very clean cut. He always wore khakis, top and bottom. At first glance, he looked to be dressed in a 1940s Army uniform.

Joe and Fannie were together so often that when you saw one, you expected to see the other. I think it was obvious to everyone that they were meant to be together. Or maybe it was Fannie who made it clear that she had a hook in Joe's jaw.

The problem was, Joe still had some carousing to do. He was a handsome fellow and a charming one. He attracted girls like bees to a pop bottle. By the spring of 1947, Fannie realized she wasn't getting all of Joe's attention. Things appeared to be completely normal during the week, but on Friday and Saturday nights, Fannie found herself home alone. Joe always had good excuses, so it took Fannie a while to figure out something wasn't quite right. In fact, Joe had an uncanny way of, as he put it, 'Not getting cetched'.

No, it couldn't be, Fannie thought to herself. *There's no way he would dare cheat on me.* On top of that, she was sure she had made it clear to everyone that Joe was off limits. There was only one way to find out, so she followed him. Fannie happened to have some prowess of her own. Her car a safe distance away, she watched as he pulled up to a girl's house. He was such a gentleman—he opened the car door for her. Then he strutted like a peacock to the other side, got in and drove away.

Fannie sat for a few minutes taking it all in. She just couldn't believe it. She had to cry for a bit. Then she removed her glasses, and the anger hit her like cold water in the face. Joe or the girl would have to pay for this; she just hadn't decided which one of them it would be. She knew where to find them. She could read Joe like a book.

Low and behold, they were at the Wheelwright movie theater, where romance was oozing from the screen. The movie was *A Night in Casablanca*. No one noticed Fannie when she strolled down the aisle to within three feet of the two lovebirds.

In a smooth motion, she took a small handgun from her purse and shot Joe in the back of the head. As shock passed over the crowd, most people thought it was an act, part of the show. But Joe and his companion certainly knew it was no act. Unchallenged by anyone, Fannie walked calmly out of the theater and drove herself home. She went to bed and thought no more about it. That is, until the next morning, when the town constable came banging on her front door.

She didn't have too much to say when the constable cuffed her and took her away. She sat without emotion until the county sheriff, who knew her, came in.

"What were you trying to do, Fannie? Don't you know you could have killed him?"

Fannie jumped to her feet. "You mean he's still alive? Well, I'll swear—I thought my aim was better than that. Next time I'll use a bigger gun."

As it turned out, the bullet had passed through the side of his neck and lodged in his left jawbone. Doctors of that day were unable, or unwilling, to remove it. So while Joe would recover, he would carry the bullet for the rest of his life.

Joe didn't press charges, so Fannie was never brought to trial for her crime of passion. They soon married and lived tumultuously ever after.

Though Joe and Floyd were identical twins, they were very different in nature. Floyd had not been drafted to serve in the war. He married a girl by the name of Hattie Collins in 1944 and lived a quiet life. He was, however, prone to moonshine whiskey from time to time, especially when Joe came around. Floyd was also known for wearing khaki. Most people couldn't tell one twin from the other, although Floyd was always a bit heavier than Joe.

The twins' view of life had without a doubt passed down from Lische, Coss, and Taube. They loved horses. The only reason they owned automobiles was because the changing of the times required it. They each traveled nearly twenty miles a day to get to work, and riding horses was not practical. But this didn't keep them from being, as they say, 'old school'.

They envied how their great-grandfather had lived off the land. Joe and Floyd loved to sneak away from their wives so they could camp, just like Grandpa had done. They usually tried to make it to Collier Rock, but it all depended on whether or not the cork stayed in the bottle till they reached their destination.

One Friday afternoon, they met at Lische's old cabin, and then headed up the trail along Spring Fork Creek. They were carrying heavy loads—and the cork had already been removed—so they stopped to rest. The trail was almost level at this point, so they sat down to rest. They passed the bottle around. After a while, they looked up at the long steep climb ahead of them and decided to unroll their sleeping bags.

They were sleeping soundly when Floyd suddenly woke to a strange sensation. He held his breath and didn't move a muscle, and then he felt it again. With a loud and mournful scream, he rolled himself down the mountain. Joe was up in a heartbeat chasing after him. When Floyd stopped, he was already out of the sleeping bag. Floyd appeared to be too frightened to speak, so Joe picked up the sleeping bag. A large copperhead fell out of it.

Joe and Floyd grew tired of paying hard-earned cash for rot-gut liquor, so they decided to make their own. The twins had no intention of selling to others. They were fairly certain they could drink everything they made. Oh sure, they might share some once in a while, but only with their closest friends.

There was an all season spring in the head of the Rocky Hollow, and it was perfect. The problem was the routine they fell into. First they would get the fire going and get the alcohol dripping fast into a glass jug. Then they would sample the finished product from time to time over a deck of cards. There was Joe, Floyd, Will Harris and their cousin Ballard Johnson. It became difficult to keep up with whose turn it was to do the sampling. This usually resulted in a brawl, which resulted in damage to the still. After a couple of weeks, they determined that it might be cheaper to buy their liquor after all.

Chapter Twenty-Nine

Every man born to the Lische Johnson family had one thing in common: they would not back down from a horse. Coss and Taube were unquestionably the best. Either of those two men could mold and shape a horse into a well-behaved animal. They had an incredible ability to teach a horse to obey with the slightest of commands. They worked or used horses much like a craftsman uses his tools.

Coss was not a large man, but even at eighty-nine, he was in no way frail. There was every reason to believe he would enjoy the same longevity as his father. He still worked, and he loved to go walking or horseback riding.

In spite of warnings from his sons, Coss insisted on caring for his own horses. In August 1949, he was attempting to put new shoes on a spirited mare. Standing behind the horse, he tapped the inside of her left rear leg. This usually made a horse raise its foot into position for shoeing. But the horse did the unexpected.

Instead of giving up her foot, she kicked. Coss caught the full force of the hoof squarely in the chest, knocking him backward. Taube heard the loud thud and rushed to his father. Coss took a few minutes to catch his breath, and then continued with the shoeing. Taube urged the old man to see a doctor, but Coss refused.

The next day, Taube asked Coss if he was feeling well. Coss said he was sore but that he would be fine. Three days later, he developed a cough, but he continued to insist he was fine. On Saturday, August 17, Taube stopped by to check on Coss, and he was dead.

Taube was a man of a more modern age, yet he had grown in his father's image and learned many things from him. When Lische died, volumes of knowledge were lost. Taube had fully intended to record his grandfather's wisdom for posterity. So when Coss died so unexpectedly, he too took a great deal of knowledge with him.

Coss would be buried next to Frankie at a cemetery near Melvin. Coss had a particular blue suit he had always liked to wear on special occasions, so it was decided that he would be buried in it. The twins were called upon to dress their grandfather for his burial. The entire family had loved and respected Coss, but Floyd and Joe had idolized him.

The twins had to face it; they had to dress their grandfather, and that was that. There was only one way to get through it—they had to get drunk. They showed up at the old man's house, sat down on the porch with a jug, and got down to business. After about an hour, they felt they were ready.

They went in to start the procedure, but they found that rigor mortis had already set in. They pulled the old man from the bed. As one held him in the upright position, the other removed his night clothes and pulled on the suit. There was absolutely no humor in this until years later, when the two re-enacted the whole thing.

Coss's death came a few months after a horrible tragedy in Prestonsburg. On June 27, a seventeen-year-old cheerleader by the name of Muriel Baldrige was walking home from a high school ballgame. Someone attacked her, and then dragged her down to the riverbank below the bridge. There she was beaten, raped, and murdered. Muriel had received five blows to the head, every one of which would have been fatal. Police found a lead pipe and an empty whiskey bottle at the scene, but her killer or killers were never caught. The murder remains an unsolved mystery.

Chapter Thirty

In the fall of 1950, Johnny was again headed for combat. The Korean peninsula had been divided at the thirty-eighth parallel, and the Communist north had invaded the south. Once again the United States and seventeen of its allies would intervene to stop the bloodshed. No one thought much of the task; a simple show of force would probably do the trick.

Major General Oliver Smith now led the First Marine Division. In October 1950, they landed at Wonsan. From there they headed north to Hagaru-ri, on the south end of the Chosin Reservoir near the border of Manchuria. Their mission was to seize the strategic hydroelectric power plant.

The Marines were holding their own against the North Korean forces, but they had a surprise coming. MacArthur had denied that the Chinese would become involved in the campaign. In fact, the Chinese had been hidden in the Taebaek Mountains, waiting for the right moment.

On the night of November 27 1950, the temperature was twenty below zero. In a blinding snowstorm, the Chinese sprung their trap. The Marines were caught off guard. With seven armored divisions totaling 120,000 troops, the Chinese had the Marines surrounded and outnumbered seven to one. The Chinese forces were under the command of General Sung Shi-Lun. He now had an opportunity to annihilate the elite First Marine Division.

Navy and Marine commanders proposed a massive airlift to evacuate the First Marine Division. This would mean leaving everything behind. But General Smith replied, "We'll fight our way out like Marines, and we'll bring our gear with us."

General Smith rallied his troops. "Marines, they're on our right, they're on our left, and they're all around us. They can't all get away this time." And when a reporter for the United Press asked General Smith via a radio interview how the retreat was going, Smith responded, "Retreat, hell! We're just attacking in another direction."

The Pentagon was not so optimistic. Washington officials had already admitted to the public that the First Marine Division was sure to be lost.

Back home, Ida was glued to the radio as tense moments turned into days and then weeks without news. She knew there could be a knock at the door at any moment. Taube had always been able to reassure her, but this time was different. He too knew that odds were they would never see Johnny alive again.

The Marines fought day and night. The Chinese were much better equipped for the mountain fighting and the bitter cold. But the Marines had one advantage; they had close air support. Marine pilots flying Corsair fighters from offshore carriers pounded targets around the clock. HO3S-1 helicopters darted in and out, evacuating the dead and wounded. The Marines had yet another aerial advantage, an elite group of Marine pilots with Panther jets. One of those elite daredevils was a young Marine, Captain John Glenn.

Miraculously, the Marines fought their way out. To the United States and its UN allies, the frozen Chosin Reservoir as it was now being called was a defeat. To the Marines, it was some of their finest hours.

In January 1951, Taube and Ida received a letter from Johnny. He had been treated for frostbite.

Ida's mind was at ease, but it was short lived. In the spring of 1951, their youngest son, Charles, was drafted into the army and on his way to the Republic of Korea. Once again, she had two sons serving in combat. Thankfully, both sons returned home safely when the war ended in 1953. Charles was honorably discharged from the army. He went back to school and became a federal mine inspector. Once again, Johnny remained in the corps.

With all her sons safe and well, it should have been happy times for Ida, but she passed away that fall. Ida had always been a strong person. There wasn't a lazy bone in her body. She was also business savvy. She raised a family and, without the help of anyone, amassed a small fortune. Ida left a legacy for all who knew her.

Just as Coss had done when he lost his wife, Taube kept himself busy. He never mentioned Ida's passing and made it clear he didn't care to discuss it. Taube had a lot to keep him occupied. He had never completely gotten out of banking. The bank now had two branches. The main office was in Prestonsburg, with a branch office in Martin. The bank was called the Bank Josephine. He had also invested in a number of businesses that made him money even as he slept.

The 1950s were rich, prosperous years for anyone willing to work and earn it. The men who had returned from the Second World War had just gotten settled when the war in Korea broke out. Now, however, there was a feeling of elation. At least for now, mothers and wives didn't have to worry about the dreaded knock at the door.

The nation was breathing again, babies were being born, and houses were being built. People were buying cars faster than Detroit could build them. The big coal companies enjoyed the spoils of war, producing millions of tons for the war effort.

In southeastern Kentucky, the big companies had, for the most part, kept their promise to the communities. They built stores and shops. They built water systems and power plants. They even built ballparks complete with bleachers and lights.

But now with the wars over, the mountains ravaged, and the money made, the big companies moved out and took it all with them. It seemed to happen overnight. One day, the theaters suddenly closed and the stores and shops became vacant buildings. While the rest of the nation enjoyed the golden, prosperous 1950s, desperate men in southeastern Kentucky looked for work. There was a mass exodus as men headed north to work the factories, with their families soon joining them.

A few small coal companies tried to survive. However, when the big companies pulled out, the railroad followed. This made it difficult for the small companies to get their coal to the market. Most of them failed in their first year.

As nature would have it, enough people had left the area to allow those who stayed behind an opportunity to survive. New and independent businesses were created. There were theaters and drive-in restaurants. People built houses and installed their own private water systems. Children went to school and played on ballparks without lights. The people of southeastern Kentucky were proving their resilience to all the world.

There was one certain conciliation: young men were not being blown apart on foreign soil. The United States was at peace. Sure, there were skirmishes among tribes in Africa, northern India, and the Suez Canal. There was some quarreling with the Russians. And the French were attempting to colonize a small country in Southeast Asia known as Vietnam.

Chapter Thirty-One

In the mid-1950s, even more of the large companies pulled out of the eastern Kentucky coal fields. What they left behind was for the poor but determined people who did not want to leave their homes.

The large coal seams close to the valley floor had been worked out. Now there were mines as narrow as twenty-eight inches being operated by men who worked entire shifts lying on their backs. They even ate their lunches lying on their backs.

The entrances of these mines were more than two thousand feet up the mountain. Trucks loaded with as much as eighty thousand pounds of coal had to navigate steep mountainous roads with hairpin turns and drop-offs. For those who drove the coal to the market, each day brought new and unexpected hazards. If air brakes failed, there was tragedy. Thick morning fog and a stopped vehicle in the road left no option for truck drivers. They drove into the side of a cliff or over one.

Working in the mines themselves was still dangerous as well. Young David Sammons was killed in a Weeksbury coal mine in 1955. In total, seven miners were killed in Pike County coal mines that year and four in Floyd County, in what miners called dust explosions. Coal dust, which was extremely flammable and ever present, often ignited or exploded. There was also the danger of completely colorless and odorless pockets of natural gas, resulting in certain death. The miners developed a rather unusual but effective detection system. They would carry a small bird or animal into the mine in a cage. If the creature died, it was proof of poisonous gas.

Christmas was one of the toughest times for the people of east Kentucky. There was an unspoken brotherhood among miners. They took up small donations among themselves in order to provide a treat for the children. The treat usually consisted of an apple, an orange, and a bag of hard candy. On the Saturday before Christmas, the entire community would turn out for the event, held at a church or ballpark.

Indeed there was a brotherhood, but there were some squabbles as well. One of those squabbles took place one morning when a group of miners were sharing coffee before the workday got under way. They were talking shop and just making small talk about making money and paying bills. Mark Smith had to be the most unusual looking individual you could imagine and he knew it. He was long, and lanky with big ears and a large Adams apple. However; the most unusual thing about him was his nose. It was long, crooked and dropped to a point at the end, much like a hawk's beak.

When someone mentioned paying bills, Mark said, "You know, my little wife is purdy and everything; she just can't hold her bill down." He was referring to her bill at the general store, but Elmer Spears saw a chance to poke a little fun.

Elmer focused his eyes on Mark's nose and asked, "Does your wife have a bill like yours, Mark?"

Mark started to grin, but when the other men began to laugh he flew into Elmer and away they went rolling through the mud. The other men managed to separate the two and the foreman assigned them separate work areas to keep them apart.

Throughout the day the two boasted about how they were going to kill each other. So convincing was their threats that all the men knew that one of them would surely die and the other would go to jail. Early that evening when the men emerged from the mine they were met with the fire warden. The fire warden had complete legal authority to summon every able-bodied man to fight forest fires and probably still does today.

The men were loaded into two trucks and taken to the fire near McDowell. Along the way Mark and Elmer snarled at each other. As ugly fate would have it the two would-be killers were assigned to the same team. Shoulder to shoulder they fought fire through the night. Just after dawn the next day the two staggered out of the woods. They were so exhausted they were practically holding each other up. The fire was under control and the two had lost their appetite for murder. They remained best friends for the rest of their lives.

Life in the coal fields wasn't all work, pain and poverty. There was recreation in the form of basketball, football and some really stiff competition in baseball. There were school carnivals and church socials. Groups of men would gather at the general store to play cards where large bets were placed. These bets were usually penny candy and sometimes all the way up to five cent candy bars. Tall tales were told during these high-stakes games.

Oscar (Awk) Thompson was one who could tell some unbelievable stories and make them sound convincing. He told of killing a twenty-one foot copperhead, which was seven times longer than the average full grown copper-head. He boasted of having the fastest rabbit dog in Floyd County, but when he and his dog came face to face with a hoop-snake the dog was no match. He said that when his dog chased and caught up with the snake, it simply took its tail into its mouth, formed a hoop and rolled away faster than the word of God.

It is a fact that a mountain lion had been seen in the area, but the cat or cats had done no harm. Although some chickens had disappeared on occasion. To the local children the mountain lion was their mystery and a reason to be indoors before dark. To them it was a ferocious beast and a reason to go to bed early, to hide under the safety of heavy quilts and tell harrowing tales. But they lost their mystery for just a day or two in the spring of 1964.

Awk Thompson spread word about the community that he had killed the mountain lion. It was broad daylight when he met up with the cat deep in the forest of Pine Fork Hollow. He said he had to shoot the animal nine times to kill it. He happened to have a tape-measure with him and he measured the cat to be nine feet, two inches from the tip of its nose to the tip of its tail. The monster was as black as coal and must have weighed five hundred pounds. This troubled the local children; they didn't want to lose their mystery. But there were issues with Awk's story that just didn't sound quite right. The cat they had seen wasn't black, nine foot long and certainly not five hundred pounds. For those reasons they launched their own investigation. They asked Awk for the exact location of the cat's remains. They went to the site and found nothing. Later that day Awk marched proudly into Hobert Mullet's general store bragging of his big game kill. Hobert had already been to the site of the kill and retrieved his cat. He calmly looked over his glasses at

Awk and said, "Awk, you didn't kill no mountain lion. You shot ol" Midnight."

Of all the great story tellers, none could compare to John C. Hall of Buckingham Mountain. He could spin fantastic yarns faster than the human brain could process them. He said he caught a catfish out of the Big Sandy River that was so big, when he pulled it from the water the level of the river dropped three inches. He went on to say, someone took a photograph of the fish and the photograph weighed ten pounds. He claimed to have owned the smartest hog in the world. When his corn began to disappear from the field he became suspicious of the sow. He stayed in the cornfield all night to catch the bandit and sure enough he was right. Just at dawn the sow grabbed a grapevine, swung across the fence into the field. She then pulled from the stalk and counted, "Three, six, nine." That was three ears of corn for each of her three pigs. She then grabbed the vine and swung back across the fence.

He told of being chased by a large bear one evening at dusk. In the nick pf time he scrambled up a tree, but the bear followed. The bear grabbed him by the leg and pulled him from the tree. They both fell to the ground and as luck would have it John landed on top of the bear. With some quick thinking he began to tickle the bear until the bear lost his breath. John happened to have a pair of wire cutters in the pocket of his coveralls. He used the cutters to trim the bear's claws and allowed him to walk away in shame.

A number of the old folks told of a gorilla that escaped from a circus in Huntington. Mountie Mullins described the animal as a Yape that had long black hair, stood ten foot tall, with long arms. She went on to say, the Yape was so big that he slapped her mule on both ends at the same time.

Tales of the gorilla spread and miners were afraid to walk to work. Enter John C. Hall. 'He wasn't afraid of no griller.' He didn't want to see the men get fired for not reporting for work so he would set an example; he went to work, business as usual. One morning he met the gorilla on a trail. He walked right up to the gorilla and faced it nose to nose where the two of them paced in a circle for about ten minutes with neither man nor beast blinking an eye. Suddenly the gorilla slapped John. John rolled about twenty feet, then got up and slapped the gorilla. The gorilla rolled about twenty feet, then got up and slapped John again. John slapped the gorilla and this continued until it became painful to John, at which time he lit his carbide lamp and set fire to the gorilla. The gorilla screamed and ran up one mountainside and down the other spreading fire as it went. All the miners were summoned to put out the forest fire; they returned to work and the gorilla was never seen again.

John would tell these fantastic stories and become angry if he thought someone doubted his honesty. John didn't lie, he just couldn't tell a lie. You see, John C. Hall was a Baptist Minister.

Chapter Thirty Two

Taube met and married a schoolteacher in 1954. She was known as Winnie B. In 1955, they had a daughter, Suzie. Winnie B. was a brilliant, well-respected woman. She would go on to become the Floyd County Schools superintendent. They were a happy and successful couple, although it's unclear how they found the time for a home life. Taube's happiest moments were the hours he spent with his horses. From the time she was able to walk, Suzie shared the same fascination. Even as a little girl, she would walk right up to the most stubborn of horses and take control.

Taube was at a stage in his life when he kept no more than four horses. For those who don't know, horses are a lot of work. And if you have superior, expensive horses, they're even more work. The barn has to be kept clean and in good working order, and the horses have to be fed, exercised, and rubbed down on a daily basis. For Taube and Suzie, it was fun work—or therapeutic, to say the least.

The year 1958 proved to be a tragic one. There had been heavy snowfall. In February, heavy downpours melted the snow, flooding every stream and river. The flood of '58 damaged or washed away homes and businesses, but that was not the greatest tragedy.

On the morning of February 28, a bus driven by twenty-seven-year-old John DeRossett was headed to the Prestonsburg School. The bus was less than a mile from Prestonsburg on winding US Highway 23. Suddenly, the bus came upon two cars and a tow truck blocking the road after a minor accident. The bus slammed into the tow truck, veered to the left, then teetered on the edge of a cliff above the swollen Big Sandy River.

The rear door was opened, and a few students were able to escape. But then the bus dropped fifty feet down onto the riverbank. Again the bus stopped, caught by a willow tree. DeRossett was seen helping children from the bus. Then the willow snapped, and the bus rolled into the river and disappeared.

The Kentucky National Guard was called in, but they were unable to locate the bus. US Navy divers were then dispatched to the scene. The bus had washed downstream. Fifty-three hours after it fell into the river, it was finally pulled from the muddy water. Twenty-two children survived; twenty-six children and the bus driver perished.

One of the businesses damaged by the flood was the Martin branch of the Bank Josephine. The most important pieces of the bank's property, such as wills and deeds, were kept at the main office at Prestonsburg. However, the cash vault at Martin had been flooded.

Taube had a unique way of dealing with the unexpected. He didn't curse or stomp his feet and ask why. He simply did what had to be done. He had to find workers who could be trusted to help clean and restore the money. The so-called paper money (which is not paper but cotton fiber) was simply washed and dried. The coins were a more difficult task. They had been packaged in paper rolls that now fell apart at the slightest touch. The coin currency was shoveled into a large barrel, where workers spent long hours sorting, cleaning, counting, and repackaging it.

In 1955, Johnny met and married a lady by the name of Georgina Hall. Georgina had grown up just on the other side of Jacks Creek Mountain in neighboring Knott County. As Johnny was away serving in the Marine Corps, few knew how their paths crossed. They had a happy marriage in spite of the fact that Johnny was a strict disciplinarian. And in spite of the difficulty of military life, Georgina wanted children, so they had two boys, Terry and Timothy.

It wasn't long before Johnny saw the writing on the wall: the situation in Vietnam would be Korea all over again. Although they had received financial assistance from the United States, the French were defeated after a four-month siege at Dien Bien Phu in 1954. Vietnam was divided at the seventeenth parallel, with the poorly equipped South Vietnamese rebels fighting to keep out the Communist North.

By the late 1950s, the United States was sending in military advisors. This time, though, they would have to do it without a certain Marine. After twenty-one years and two major wars, Master Sergeant Johnny Johnson was coming home.

Johnny bought one of the four mansions coal company officials had built in a straight row high on a hill overlooking Weeksbury. A winding dirt road led to the houses. Johnny's house was at the end of the road. It was the lesser of the rather elaborate homes, and it had fallen into disrepair. But the view was astounding. His cousin Hazadore, or Haz, had some adolescent aged children willing to help with the painting and the fix-up. It didn't take long until Johnny's family moved in.

Anyone who has retired from the military will tell you it's not enough for a comfortable living. It was a reliable monthly income, however, and at forty-two, Johnny was still young, healthy, and able to work. He took a job driving the school bus to supplement his military pay.

Every kid in the neighborhood looked up to Johnny and thought he was a hero. They didn't know just how much of a hero he really was, and he never mentioned it. Johnny came home with a military-surplus jeep and an M1 Garand rifle. The local kids were awestruck when Johnny would drive that four-wheel-drive jeep straight up steep hills. And when he would fire the M1, the kids thought it was the loudest and most powerful gun in the world. His sons wanted to be Boy Scouts, so Johnny became a Scoutmaster. Although he was strict a disciplinarian, but he was also as fair and honest as a man could be.

Johnny drove the bus for about two years, until one day he got a letter from an old friend who had also retired from the corps. The friend had taken a job as a prison warden in Lebanon, Ohio, near Cincinnati. There was an opening, and he wanted to hire Johnny. So in 1961, Johnny moved his family to Lebanon and became a prison guard.

Before he left he visited his relatives to say goodbye. He drove to his cousin Haz Johnson's to say goodbye where he received an unexpected send off. Two of the Johnson boys had cut down a hickory tree and peeled off a section of bark about two feet wide and six feet long. The inside of the bark was wet and very slippery. They took the bark about six hundred feet up the mountain where the eldest boy of nine sat in front while the younger boy age seven sat behind. At that same moment down in the yard Johnny was stepping out of his car. The boy in front pulled the front end of the bark upward much like a sled runner. In the meantime down below Johnny was raising his hand in greeting. With a loud 'Yeeeeeee-haaaaaaa' down the mountain the boys flew just under the speed of sound. The boys bounced high as they passed over bumps with arms and legs flying in the air, stopping only when they splashed into the creek.

Johnny, who still had one foot in the car fell to his knees with laughter still attempting to greet the boy's mother. To the boy's mother it was nothing unusual; just another day. Johnny would make another attempt to say something, but fall into another fit of laughter. He finally got back into his car and with a weak wave of his hand he drove away. He would have to come back and say goodbye later.

Now and then, Taube would share stories he had heard of Johnny's heroic exploits at the prison. If an inmate became unruly, Johnny would go in with his judo and karate hand-to-hand combat training and quiet the prisoner. Aside from those stories, though, Johnny faded from the picture.

Chapter Thirty-Three

Old Floyd raised his family not in the way Coss had raised him but more in the nature of his Grandfather Lische. Floyd raised his family to believe that having an education meant knowing how to handle livestock and grow a garden.

His son Hazadore was more like him than any of the other nine children. Both Floyd and Haz believed in having large families, with the children becoming a part of the workforce, thereby creating somewhat of a social security.

Hazadore married Ida Mae Rice. By the mid-1950s, they already had a large family. In 1954, Haz was injured in a coal mine and had to have back surgery. After that, he was unable or unwilling to work in the mine. He moved his family into the house Coss had left behind and continued to grow his family. He was determined to live the way his fathers before him had lived—unwilling to accept the changing of the times.

They were a poor but happy family. The children had endless room to run, play, and grow.

The site was now called Shop Hollow because of the machine shop at its entrance, although some still called it Lische Hollow. It was a place right out of a fairy tale. It was an incredibly green valley with pasture land and lots of garden space. At night, it was deep and dark. There were no streetlights; the only light was from the moon and stars. It was a spectacular sight when on clear nights you could see every star and even every shooting star.

It was a beautiful place to raise a family, but it was secluded with the house tucked into the head of the hollow. There had once been six houses in the hollow, all of which had been occupied by Lische and his descendants. By the end of the 1950s, there were only two homes remaining. Coss's house, where Haz and his family lived, and the original cabin Lische had built one hundred years earlier, which was occupied by Floyd and Lina.

Electrical lines were installed to the two houses. In those days, that only meant a screw-in lightbulb in each room and a socket with a plug for the radio. Haz had the pioneer spirit of his great-grandfather. He could have lived without electricity and fancy gadgets. In fact, the family had a television set before they owned a refrigerator. You see, they got the used TV in 1959 as payment for some work they had done for Johnny.

The TV was a fascinating thing for them. The metal console was large and heavy. It was supposed to resemble maple wood; the thing was just a little lighter in color than peanut butter. In spite of the console size, it had a small round screen. One of the younger children said the most fascinating thing about it was the small pale-blue light that remained in the center of the screen long after the set had been turned off.

It took amazing feats of engineering just to get a signal on it. It started with a twenty-foot length of ribbon wire that stretched to a makeshift antenna on a post in the yard. That resulted in the occasional reception of channel 3, broadcasting out of Huntington, West Virginia.

If a friend or neighbor had owned a TV longer, then that automatically made them experts. Therefore, everyone who came along had a new suggestion on how to make it work. Almost every piece of advice was followed.

The next step was to move the antenna five hundred feet or so up the mountain. Now when the weather was clear, they could pick up channel 13 from Charleston, West Virginia. The wire for this five-hundred-foot stretch consisted of two shiny copper-clad conductors with pencil-sized solenoid spacers about a foot apart. The signal came in great—until the bare wire tarnished.

Another problem occurred when a tree branch would drop on the wire, breaking the spacers and separating the conductors. To repair this problem, a carbide lamp was used to melt and fuse the conductors back together.

Then another neighbor said that if the antenna were higher on the mountain, they would get more channels. Therefore, another five hundred feet of wire was added. This resulted in channel 5 from Bluefield, West Virginia. Someone else suggested the higher the better, so the antenna was placed on the highest peak at three thousand feet, and WKYT in Lexington appeared. (Sometimes.)

The children didn't care whether or not the TV worked. They had other things to keep them occupied. They had animals to care for; including a large white workhorse they called Tony. The horse performed all the tasks expected of a workhorse, but he was more of a pet.

One morning two of the little boys were given the dreaded white sidewall haircut. This gave them the notion that Tony needed a haircut as well. They climbed to the top of the fence and onto the horse's back with a pair of scissors. The horse stood still and obedient for the haircut. When the boys were done, Tony no longer had his beautiful long white mane.

Tony was a well-trained animal; he didn't require a great deal of direction. A sled was more useful than a wagon for harvesting or hauling coal or wood, so Haz took the horse and sled to a small mine called a coal bank located just down the hollow. The smaller children always enjoyed going along for the ride. If Haz became distracted or busy doing something else, Tony was trusted to take the sled and the children and go on home.

Once when the family was out with the sled, Young Floyd came by in a brand new, shiny black 1960 Buick. He left the car parked in the road and got out to visit with Haz. The two men were deep in conversation when Tony decided to take the sled and the kids on home. It was a tight squeeze around that car, but Tony was sure he could make it. He did, but the side of the sled peeled the shiny trim right off and left a gouge the entire length of the car.

A couple of weeks later, with the car all fixed up and shiny, Young Floyd came to visit again. You would think that after the first episode, he would have been more careful. Tony had a pasture, but he often just meandered about the yard and didn't go to the barn until he was told to do so. While Floyd and Haz sat on the porch telling tall tales and reminiscing, Tony wandered over to the car. He just couldn't believe his eyes. He was looking at his reflection in the car, and he did not like what he was seeing. Who was this intruder? He began pounding the reflection with both front feet.

Floyd ran screaming, but it was too late—more bodywork would be needed.

The family had another pet. He was a large caramel-colored dog, so they called him Carmel. He was a mutt, but he was probably related to a golden retriever. He was a faithful and gentle companion for the children and followed them everywhere they went. If the children stayed out playing all day, then Carmel stayed out all day as well.

It was a warm late summer day. Haz was working in the garden farther up the hollow and just out of sight. The children were about a hundred yards up the mountain, playing in the pasture. Eight-year-old Marie was the first to notice the dog wasn't with them. She saw Carmel laying in the yard and called to him. The dog jumped up growling and snarling, and then started in their direction. Mae happened to be on the front porch and realized in an instant the dog was rabid. She began to scream for the children to climb a tree. The dog then turned and headed for her, but the frightened children were screaming louder, so the dog turned on them again.

Haz came running. The only phrase he could make out in the midst of all the screaming was 'Mad dog'. As he passed the barn, he grabbed a steel pipe about ten feet long and two inches in diameter. As he approached, the dog charged him.

The children were screaming, "Don't hurt him!"

Haz didn't want to hurt him, so he pushed the dog away with the pipe. The dog charged again and again, becoming more and more vicious with every turn. For anyone who has never seen a mad dog, it is a sight and a sound you'd never forget. They emit a sound that is a cross between a grunt and a growl. They are likely to be torn ragged and bloody.

Now fearing for his own life, Haz shoved the dog as far as he could. Before the dog could recover, Haz raised the pipe high above his head and sent it crashing down on the dog. The blow had been intended for the head, but it missed, probably breaking the dog's back instead.

The dog whimpered a soft sound, growled, and kept coming on its belly. Haz swung again, catching the dog squarely in the side of the head. This time, the dog was stunned enough to allow for a final and fatal blow.

Needless to say, the family was traumatized, but this was only the beginning. For the remainder of the summer and fall, rabies was an epidemic. Russel Hall and Ken Ray of Weeksbury died of the disease. Stories were told of unimaginable suffering and the horrible death that took them. Animals, especially dogs, acting in any way out of the ordinary were destroyed immediately. People didn't even trust their small indoor pets. It was a community living in fear.

About a month after Carmel's death, the Johnson children were walking home from their grandfather's cabin about a half mile away. They didn't realize it, but a large black dog was coming up fast behind them. Haz had a brother, Calvin, who lived near the mouth of the hollow. Mae had asked Calvin's wife, Goldie, to look after things while she went to a doctor's appointment. Goldie saw what was happening just in time.

As often was the case, Goldie had no time to go into the house for a gun. She yelled for the children to run for the safety of a small corn-crib. Without any regard for her own life, she ran out with nothing but a broom. She managed to intercept the dog just in time. Goldie had the presence of mind not to strike the dog; she merely nudged him from his course. The disease had advanced enough that the dog simply continued in the direction she had pointed him.

At the height of the epidemic, the children all told tales of hearing mad dogs as they passed the house at night. They said the sound would be very, very low at first, and then it would become louder and louder as the dog came closer. The sound would be loudest as the dog passed the house, then begin to fade again. Considering the children had experienced the trauma of seeing their dog suddenly go mad and then killed right before their eyes, these sounds could have been from nightmares or imaginations. Or they could have been real.

Time doesn't heal all wounds, but it does eventually soften the pain. Summer and fall passed, and the cold weather lessened the odds of rabies.

Chapter Thirty-Four

The 1960s soon arrived with new promises and new inventions. It was a time of the nuclear age, of new gadgets, and things of almost science fiction. Children were taught to 'Duck and Cover'. This of course was in the event of a nuclear strike. Little did we know just how futile it would have been to duck and cover. Yet people still dug bunkers in their backyards and stocked them with nonperishable food items. They looked at their neighbors who hadn't dug a bunker and thought, "Don't expect me to share." Little did they know there would have been nothing to crawl out to when their food and water were gone.

In the summer of 1960, people were told to watch the sky beginning on the evening of August 12th. A new invention would be streaking across the night sky just after dark. Moving very, very fast, it would be brighter than a star, and it would transmit voices to various places on the planet. That sounded like the most incredible thing ever. It was a new invention called a satellite. Newly formed NASA called it Echo 1.

In 1962, Floyd and Lina quit Shop Hollow and moved into the village. Haz had always wanted Shop Hollow to himself, and now he had it. He immediately tore down the old cabin Lische had built more than a hundred years before. When it came to removing the logs, the ax marks were just as prevalent as they had been when Lische and his brothers put them in place so many years before. The dovetailed corners still showed the skill of the craftsmen who meticulously cut them to fit.

On December 15, 1967, Haz was repairing the TV antenna wire somewhere up the mountain. The moment he succeeded, channel 3 came into focus with a news bulletin. A bridge crossing the Ohio River from Point Pleasant, West Virginia to Gallipolis, Ohio, had collapsed. The Silver Bridge, as it was called, fell into the muddy waters of The Ohio River, at about four p.m. The bridge had been loaded with rush hour traffic as well as Christmas shoppers. Thirty-five cars fell with the bridge. Forty-six people died, two of whom were never recovered.

By 1967, Suzie had developed her equestrian skills to the point where she needed better facilities. She wanted to race in competition, but the family really didn't need the prize money. Besides that, Taube didn't want to invest in a horse and risk losing a million dollars with one broken leg.

He did, however, invest a hundred thousand on a relative of a Kentucky Derby winner. She was a sleek, solid black three-year-old filly, and Suzie named her Annie. She was always jumpy and stubborn, but she could run like a greyhound. At full gallop, all four hooves appeared as if they would tangle beneath her, then she would stretch out and appear to double in length. Taube would settle for blue ribbons and trophies. Therefore, he taught Suzie and trained their horses for gated competition.

Suzie still wanted better facilities. She wanted a large area with a four-board oak fence, where the horses could graze and sun themselves during the day. Then she wanted a competition-size oval training ring. She wanted locust posts with one by six rough sawn oak lumber.

Taube knew exactly where he would get the fence posts. His nephew Haz had three teenaged sons who were always looking for work. The one by six lumber he would get at the mill, but he asked the boys to cut three hundred fence posts eight feet in length. He also hired the boys to help build the fence.

Taube's house was within rock-throwing distance of the Melvin Wye. Route 122 runs through Melvin, and right in the center of town, Route 466 branches off toward Weeksbury. On the other side of the Wye was a small restaurant called the Little Wye Drive-In. The Little Wye was a fun place with a jukebox that sent the hits echoing through the mountains. Young people came from all around to visit the Little Wye. It was a place to have fun, fight, get arrested, or just be stupid. Haz's boys would be working for Taube through the whole summer. It would be a fun-filled time, and the Little Wye would keep things interesting.

Taube also hired Old Joe's grandson, Donnie, along with a local boy by the name of William Dewy Osborn. Donnie was eighteen years old, good nature, hardworking, but a little boisterous. William pulled his weight as well, but he was working for one thing and one thing only: moonshine whiskey.

The crew set fenceposts the first week. When Saturday came, Taube paid them. Knowing Donnie to be the wild one, Taube put his hand on Donnie's shoulder and asked his great-nephew: "What are you going to do with your money, Don?"

Donnie said, "Well, I'm going to fill up my car, and I'm going to go out and get drunk."

"You'll break your damn fool neck," Taube said.

Monday morning, the crew was back on the job, but there was no Donnie. One of the boys asked Taube if he knew where Donnie was.

"About twelve miles down that road, he rolled his car," Taube said. "He died of a broken neck."

It was to be a summer of death in eastern Kentucky. James Hall was killed at noon on June 9 in Weeksbury. Just a freak accident; he was a passenger in a 1964, Falcon convertible with his sister-in-law driving. The car flipped once to the side, pinning him. He died instantly.

Taube had also warned William Dewy that he was killing himself with alcohol. About six weeks later, William Dewy failed to show up for work. Later that day, word came. A neighbor had gone to check on him and found him dead. The autopsy revealed traces of drain cleaner in his stomach. It was believed that the bootlegger had used the chemical to unplug the worm, a coil of copper tubing where steam from the boiling ingredients condenses to form alcohol. William Dewy didn't just find some bad whiskey; he found some poisoned whiskey.

The Wheelwright ballpark was within sight of where the boys were working. Saturdays and Sundays drew large crowds for softball or baseball competition. There was never enough parking, and people had to park on the shoulder of the road. Haz's boys were accustomed to being in the quiet surroundings of Shop Hollow. With all the traffic and noise, it was like a window onto the world.

But one Saturday morning in July would prove to be tragic. A family parked in the long line of cars on the shoulder of the road. When their seven-year-old daughter stepped from between two cars into the roadway, she was killed instantly.

A near-tragedy occurred when a group of young people gathered on a Saturday morning by the gas station in front of Taube's house. They were passing a loaded .22-caliber pistol around, checking the feel and the balance. The boys were aiming the gun; discussing the range and accuracy at various distances. The pistol likely belonged to a twenty-year-old by the name of Danny Ray Collins. When the gun was passed back to him, he twirled it on his forefinger, cowboy style. The pistol discharged, striking Danny in the left side just below the ribcage. Danny's wound was not serious, but he learned a lesson about playing with a loaded gun.

Every community has at least one of these: a town drunk, a village idiot, and a bully. This community had a man who wore the hats of all three. We'll just call him Mack. We won't mention his last name because he had come from good folks. He had lots of relatives who were good and law-abiding citizens. The sad thing about it was that he was the family patriarch. In other words, he should have been old enough to know better.

The night brings out the vampires; the full moon brings out the werewolves. But this fellow's demons came right out of the bottle. He was a decent guy, sensible and accommodating, until he removed that cork. He was a known loan shark. A number of people in the area were glad to get a small payday loan from him. But that's not the worst of it. The problem was, the terms of such loans were verbal and easy for Mack to alter. He would make a loan to some poor, unsuspecting fool, and within two to three days, he would demand payment in full with interest. And he made the demand with a gun in his hand. If he came calling and the man of the house was not at home, the missis was often fondled—or worse.

Mack made a loan to one of Haz's sons, and then showed up at three in the morning with a pistol in his hand. He forced the twenty-three-year-old newlywed into his truck. They drove about a mile to the boy's boss for the money. The boss was Orville Olney.

Of the three of Haz's sons working for Taube, it was neither the oldest nor the youngest but the one in the middle who reacted the most to Mack's exploits. He made it clear to his family that if Mack entered their home with a gun, he would not leave alive.

One summer morning, the sixteen-year-old was awakened by his older sister Lily.

"Mack's downstairs—he has a pistol, and he's sitting beside our father on the couch."

"Which side is he sitting on?" the boy asked. "Is he sitting next to the corner, or next to the door?"

"He's sitting next to the door." She responded.

"Is the shotgun loaded?"

"Yes," she said. "I loaded it myself."

It was not stairs but more of a ladder that led from the loft where the boy had been sleeping. Lily had placed the shotgun at the bottom of the ladder. From there, two steps would take the boy into the living room and not much more than twelve feet from Mack. It would be an easy shot.

A million thoughts raced through his mind as he climbed down that ladder. He knew there would be consequences. He knew the bloody mess a shotgun would make at close range. But all this would have to be sorted out later. For now, he would save his family. What he knew for certain was at sixteen years of age, he was about to end a man's life.

As he reached the bottom of the ladder, his mother had already picked up the shotgun and was walking out the backdoor. He followed her.

"What are you doing?" he demanded.

"You leave Mack alone," she responded. "Your father knows how to handle a drunk."

The boy was confused, but he was obedient enough to be humbled by his mother's words. After about an hour, Mack left without incident.

Mack's behavior continued for a good number of years, until a Saturday morning in late summer 1970. The boys and Taube were working, and Suzie was doing some grooming. Beyond the two-lane Highway 122 was a gravel frontage road, then a row of houses. The sound of two men arguing loudly caught everyone's attention. They knew in an instant it was Mack attempting to collect; his truck was parked in front of one of the houses.

Mack walked out of the house. "I'm going down the road for a few minutes," he said, looking over his shoulder as he approached his truck. "When I come back, you had better pay me."

Just then, a man by the name of Billy Harrington stepped out on to the porch and yelled, "I'm going to pay you now, Mack!"

With that, he shot Mack in the side of the head with a shotgun.

Mack's hat must have flown thirty feet in the air and landed in the weeds. Mack hit the ground like a ball of wet mud.

The ambulance crew came about a half hour later and hauled him away. Mack survived the shooting, but he lost his left eye. He was also forever cured of the urge to bully.

Chapter Thirty-Five

Back in 1952, Young Floyd bought about two hundred acres of land with good timber, coal, and water. A few years later, he cut enough timber from the land to build a log cabin. The cabin was built to resemble the one from Bonanza, a TV western. There was a good view of Weeksbury, so he added a wraparound porch, where he could watch the world go by.

Floyd had a good job with Island Creek Coal Company, where he had worked for more than twenty years. His was a surface job at the large coal-processing plant at Price. He bought a new car every two years and appeared to be the man who had everything. Floyd and Hattie were a happy couple, but what they wanted most they couldn't have. Floyd and Hattie wanted children more than anything on Earth, but they were unable to have them.

Then there was a strange twist of fate in 1964. Hattie's brother, Hoss Collins, and his wife, Grace, divorced. During the bitterness of the separation, their two children, Patricia and Emil, stayed with Hattie and Floyd. When things settled down between the two, it was time for the children to leave. However, Floyd and Hattie begged Hoss and Grace to let the children stay. The children begged to stay as well. Hoss and Grace agreed, and it became permanent.

Pat was the oldest. She grew up to be a voluptuous blonde with dark-green eyes. She was loud but witty and fun to be around. Emil was always clean, well dressed, and well provided for. For this reason, he was thought to be a sissy.

In the spring of 1968, Emil finished high school, turned eighteen, and registered for the draft. Two months later, while he was pondering college decisions, he was drafted.

The way Floyd and Hattie reacted to his being drafting, was as if the boy had already been killed. No one had ever suffered the way those two people suffered. It all happened so quickly. They constantly asked themselves what they could have done differently to alter or somehow manipulate fate itself.

But Floyd and Hattie knew there was no changing the fact that Emil had to serve. All they could do was cross their fingers and hope for the best. After all, not every boy who was drafted was sent to Vietnam. Emil had finished high school; they had heard that mostly dropouts were serving on the ground in Vietnam. And, the United States had bases all over the world. Perhaps he would even be stationed stateside and they could visit him at the base.

All these good and positive possibilities were removed one by one. Emil completed eight weeks of basic training, and then he came home for ten days. While Emil was catching up on some much-needed rest, Hattie stole a look at some of his papers. She quickly scanned them until she saw 'MOS 03'. She knew the MOS stood for Military Occupational Specialty. It was a system for categorizing the different career fields in the military. But she needed to find out what the 03 meant. That was Emil's job code. If anyone knew, it would be her brother-in-law Johnny. Hattie frantically dug through the drawer for his number.

Georgina answered and heard the urgency in Hattie's voice as she asked to speak to Johnny. "Is everything all right?" Georgina asked.

"I'm not sure," Hattie replied. "I need to ask Johnny a military question."

Anxious seconds ticked by as she waited for Johnny to come to the phone. When Johnny answered, Hattie wasted no time.

"What does 03 mean?" she blurted.

There was a long, silent pause. Then Johnny answered with one word: "Infantry."

He went on to say, "But listen, Hattie, that doesn't necessarily mean Vietnam. We're still at odds with the Russians. Emil could be stationed in Germany."

Infantry. Hattie was unable to speak. She just hung up the phone.

Emil left for another six weeks of Advanced Infantry Training. Hattie and Floyd prayed that Johnny was right about Emil possibly being stationed elsewhere. They asked all their friends and neighbors to pray as well.

In September 1968, Emil came home once again for another ten-day leave. They gazed at his papers. There was a long military address, but all they could see were the last few words: Saigon, South Vietnam. Days later, he said goodbye and he was on his way.

While Emil was away, Floyd and Hattie rushed to the post office each day. Hattie raced in with her hands squeezed together, fingers interlocked in prayer, that they would get a letter from him. If they didn't, they wept mournfully. If they did, they would race to Haz and Mae's, where the family gathered and listened as Hattie read each letter aloud.

In fact, they visited Haz and Mae every day while Emil was in Vietnam. They just needed somewhere to go and someone to be with. Haz, Mae, and the entire Johnson family shared Floyd's and Hattie's sadness.

For thirteen months, Emil would be in some of the most hellish fighting of the war. The long days of the war were almost as agonizing for Floyd and Hattie as they were for Emil. To them, every day was or could be Emil's funeral. She broke down completely when one of Emil's letters described the sick feeling a man gets when he has just killed another human being.

Whether it was due to all the poignant prayers or another twist of fate, Emil came home in the fall of 1969. Like anyone fortunate enough to have survived such an ordeal, he was a changed man.

Chapter Thirty-Six

Of the three Johnson boys who worked for Taube, the one in the middle was, to say the least, a little different. He wasn't a bad-looking boy, and he wasn't a bad-natured boy. His intelligence was at least average, but there were times when he just didn't use his head. He would often formulate some grand plan in his head and make every attempt to carry it out—even after someone of greater authority made every effort to convince him the plan wouldn't work. At times, he was a dunce.

When he was about six years old he over-heard his older brother, Ernie say to someone, "There's a pot of gold at the end of every rainbow."

So, the next time he saw one, off he went. He ran, stumbling and falling as he traveled over hill and dell, never taking his eyes off the guiding rainbow. When he finally got there, he was bewildered to find that his pot of gold had turned into a great big chestnut tree stump. The only solution he could come up with was that his pot of gold must be buried beneath that stump.

However, since he was already exhausted he decided to ask his brother before digging up the site. Fortunately, his brother was kind enough to tell him it was only a myth.

He once found a foreign object hidden in a closet. He marched into the living room, where his mother was visiting with a friend. "What in the devil is this?" he asked, holding it up.

His younger brother quickly ushered him into the other room. "Just leave things alone if you don't know what they are!" his brother said. "A man who doesn't use his head may as well have an ass on both ends." The dunce didn't realize it was feminine protection.

To his credit, the boy had a curiosity to learn. He watched Taube's every move, and he learned from his brothers. He also followed his father as often as he could on his many hunting trips. They traveled for miles and hunted through the night.

In late October 1970, one of their excursions took them to a deep and uninhabited hollow known as the Crooked Branch. That day they were hunting not for game animals but ginseng. Looking for ginseng was somewhat of a sport in those days. They sold the valuable root to The RT Greer herb Company of Pikeville and the money was used to pay small debts. The ginseng plant is different from any other. In the fall, it becomes a beautiful gold in color with a pod of bright red berries extending above the top of the plant.

By late afternoon, they made their way to the bottom of the hollow and drank from a clear running stream. Haz gave him this warning: "There's already been a killing frost. Do you see those places up there on that hillside where the sun is shining through the trees?" He pointed. "Well, that's where we're going. And if there's a snake to be found, he'll be there warming himself in the sun."

The boy was daydreaming at the time, but he would soon wake up. They were making their way around the steep side of the mountain, hacking at grapevines and stinging nettles, when they broke into the bright autumn sunlight. There, about two feet off the ground, lying in the vines, was a large copperhead taking aim at his father's leg.

"We're in a copperhead den!" the boy screamed just in time.

"Where?" Haz yelled.

"They're all around us!" the boy said, seeing snakes everywhere he looked. There were too many to count.

As quick as lightning, Haz shot the snake closest to him. But it was only a single-shot gun, and there was no time to reload. Haz jabbed away with the butt of the gun while the boy hacked away with his walking stick. It was impossible to run through the brush and the vines, so they had to stand their ground and fight for their lives.

When it finally appeared to be over, Haz said they should turn around and go back the way they came.

"Wait a minute," the boy said. "There's a snake coiled in some ferns about forty feet back. We passed it along the way."

Haz loaded the shotgun, found and killed the snake. Confused, he asked, "Do you mean we walked right past that snake the first time, and you didn't say anything? Why?"

"I honestly don't know," the boy said. "I truly believe that devil charmed me!"

That would not be the boy's last encounter with snakes. In June 1971, he went camping atop Collier Rock with five members of the Mullet family: Rick, Roy, Dennis, Tony, and Gordon. It was well after dark, and the boys were sharing stories.

Rick said to the boy, "You and your father know just about everything there is to know about these mountains, don't you?"

This inflated the boy's ego. "Sure we do. I've got a spot where I could hide right here on the top of this plateau, and you'd never find me."

Oh yeah?" Rick said. "I'd like to see you try."

With that, the Johnson boy and two of the Mullets went off to the secret hiding place. The other boys would wait for a couple of minutes, and then try to find them.

The hiding spot was only about a hundred feet from where young Abe Hampton had swung over the cliff on a vine many years earlier. That fact alone should have been enough of an omen. The Johnson boy led the Mullets to a small cavity under a large rock no more than two feet from the edge of the cliff. Its opening was just big enough to hide the three boys. The dunce went in first, and the two Mullet boys came in behind, all of them facing the edge of the cliff.

The instant they sat down, the boy heard a soft *ch-ch-ch-ch* sound. "We're in a rattlesnake den!" he cried out to the others. But the Mullet boys thought he was only trying to frighten them so they just giggled.

The Johnson boy pushed hard against their backs. "I mean it! If you don't get going, I'm gonna push you over the cliff!" They all scrambled to safety just in time.

When the other boys arrived, they had a flashlight. They shone the light deep into the opening of the hiding space. To their horror, they saw dozens of small rattlesnakes about a foot long, knotted and crawling on the very spot where the boys had just been. And keep in mind: small snakes don't give a warning rattle. Although they have their venom, their rattle doesn't begin to form for a full year.

The next day, the boy told his story to his brothers Jimmy, Charles, Deanie, and his uncles Calvin and IB. All of them listened skeptically. They denied the possibility of snakes atop Collier Rock. None of them had ever seen as much as a harmless snake up there, let alone rattlesnakes. There were far too many visitors in the area—too much noise and confusion and too many campfires.

They did, however, think the boy's story should at least be investigated. They gathered some blasting materials and set out to see for themselves. The dunce was eternally grateful to be accompanied on this trip. They could help him with something that nearly cost him his life. Deannie, Calvin, and IB were coal miners with extensive skills in blasting, and it would come in handy.

They each took turns peering into the opening. To the dunce's dismay, none of them saw a single snake.

Calvin attempted to let the embarrassed boy down easy. "Well, I was afraid you were mistaken. I told you I've never seen a snake on top of these rocks."

The boy stood his ground. "I know what I saw, Uncle Calvin."

They were just about to leave when IB said, "Boys, I see a rattlesnake right back under this bolder." He had been walking around, looking for potential places where snakes might be hiding.

Everyone ran excitedly to have a look. Sure enough, about ten feet back under a large rock was roughly four inches of a snake's body exposed. The boy felt like jumping for joy. Suddenly, Uncle IB was his hero.

Now with proof, they carefully set dynamite charges and blasted every place where a snake could hide. Again, it was IB who was the first to find bits and pieces of the snakes when they were finished.

Chapter Thirty-Seven

On the first Sunday of September 1971, the Johnson family held a long overdue family reunion. The gathering would take place on the spot Lische had chosen for a garden high above the creek and safe from flooding. It was perfect. It was a grassy pasture with ample shade along the edge of the forest. A large tent was set up.

People came all the way from Martin County. There must have been at least a hundred people. It was a fun-filled event with horseshoes and lawn darts and just about any kind of food and drink you could imagine. Non-alcoholic, of course, Haz would never have allowed alcohol.

The joyous event ended at about four in the afternoon. The boy felt a deep sadness he couldn't understand. Was it because the happy reunion everyone had been looking forward to for so long was over? Was it because he'd never see many members of that picnic again?

He took a stroll that eventually led him to the top of Collier Rock. The evening was fast approaching when he sat down at what Lische had called the eastern lookout. The sky was turning dark as night crept in from the east. Somewhere far below, a whippoorwill had already started its dusk-till-dawn call.

I've got to know what's out there, he said to himself. *I want to see big cities and the mighty Atlantic Ocean. And after that, I want to turn around and go to the Pacific. I want to see the Gulf of Mexico and the Gulf of Maine. I want to see the cold north woods of Canada and maybe some places across the sea.*

It must have been a premonition. A few days later, on September 9, his brother Ernie called from Springfield, Ohio, with an offer for a job.

The adventure began.

Epilogue

If you'll remember, Buddy Ed Rice was crushed in a mine cave-in back in 1926. His wife, Eveline, died just seven months later, leaving the children alone in the world. Little Jim Rice was one of the children. He lived to be forty, dying from cancer in 1962. His younger sister, Ida Mae Rice, grew up and married Haz Johnson. They had thirteen children.

I, Wynn, am one of them. I'm the dunce.

My mother lived to see her eighty-fourth birthday in February 2008 and died one hour after it ended. When her father, Buddy, died he had twenty-seven cents and a can of tobacco in his pockets. My mother kept those items; they were among her most treasured possessions.

Taube's son Floyd died of a heart attack in 1975. Hattie lived for another nine years; she died in 1984. Taube's son Johnny died in 1978 from cancer. He was buried with full military honors. It took nearly an hour to read of his heroics.

Taube's brother Floyd, my grandfather, had never been sick a day in his life. In February 1979, he was eighty-eight and going strong, but then he died suddenly from an aneurysm. It would be weeks before I would learn of my grandfather's death. I was a Marine serving on a Navy ship off the north coast of Africa. After his death, my grandmother Lina complained that he came back to her in the night. She said Floyd would sit on the bed and talk to her. If she tried to ignore him, he would pull the covers from the bed and leave her cold. Although she had enjoyed relatively good health as well, she only outlived Floyd by three months. She died in May 1979.

Taube's brother Joe and his wife, Liza, both died in 1979, as did Monk Hall, Taube's brother-in-law. Monk's wife, Dine, had passed years before, in 1964. Floyd and Lina's eldest son Chris died suddenly of an aneurysm in 1980. Their second-born son, Hazadore, died from artery disease just three years later in 1983. He was my father.

Joe and Fannie had a long, successful, but rocky marriage. Joe had finagled his uncle (Old Joe) into selling the house and land on the mountain. Old Joe and Liza moved into a small house at the bottom of the hill not far from Monk and Dine. Fannie passed away in the fall of 1983, giving Joe the freedom to carouse. In fact, he caroused himself to death—he died a year later.

I wrote this book from my memories of the true stories my great-uncle Taube told me. He once said to me, "I've seen the transition from the horse and buggy to the space shuttle." Taube was a fascinating man. I was one of the boys who worked for him, along with my brothers Charles and Jimmy Johnson. Taube was kind and generous to us, and we loved him dearly.

In 1968, Taube purchased eighty acres of land just outside of Prestonsburg. The land was located along Abbott Creek. At eighty-two years of age, he was not finished making money. He asked the Johnson boys to walk the land and determine whether he had made a good purchase. We found it to contain a virgin forest, including groves of tall, straight poplar. More importantly, we found cool running springs of water. This meant the coal was still under the land.

Taube made a deal with a small excavating company to look for coal. They found not just coal but Kindle-coal. Kindle-coal is a hard, shiny coal with extremely high coal-oil content. It ignites easily, burns cleaner and emits more heat than common coal. In the first year of operation, the mine grossed just over three million dollars. I think Taube was determined to make money till the day of his funeral.

Sometime in the late 1970s, his wife, Winnie, decided it would be best for them to move to Prestonsburg. Taube was never happy there. He longed for the home he had built so many years before. He longed for his horses and his barn. His life finally began to wane. Then one day, he was committed to a nursing home.

Taube had amassed a fortune in his time. He loved to make money and he loved to hold money. One day, he asked that some of his money be brought to him—he wanted to know he still owned it. The staff at the nursing home presented him with a stack of money from a Life game, but he was not to be fooled. He knew it was play money.

Taube had nicknames for the three of us boys who worked for him. My nickname was Skyball, for whatever the reason. Taube died in the fall of 1989, just before his hundred and fourth birthday. He was nearly the same age as his grandfather when he passed. They tell me that on his death-bed he asked to see Skyball. I don't remember where I was or what I was doing, but it was not to be.

About the Author

My name is Wynn Johnson. I was born on June 28, 1954 in a small hospital in Virgie, Kentucky. Today, locals would argue there is no hospital in Virgie. That's because shortly after I was born the wooden structure burned to the ground and was never rebuilt.

I spent the first seventeen years of my life growing up in the east Kentucky coal fields. I'm fairly certain that had I stayed there, I could have been happy and probably made a modest living. The problem with that, though, was my nagging spirit for adventure and that's what life has been for me- a grand and glorious adventure.

On Friday April 15, 1968, my brothers Charles, Jimmy and I were camping at our favorite campsite atop Colliers Rock. As we lay on our blanket rolls looking up into a cloudless night and a full moon, we talked about the future and what we would be when we grew up.

I remember saying, "You know, I think I'm going to be seeing that old moon from a lot of different angles in the world."

Charles then said, "No, I don't think so, Wynn. You'll probably be right here with the rest of us." Well fate had another plan in mind for me, for I have traveled to many places and seen many different cultures and ways of life. Of the things I treasure most, are the memories of the many wonderful people I've met along the way. My ability to tell stories comes from a life of travel and my passion for books.

I have read many books and I guess my love for reading was developed while serving as a Marine at sea with the Navy. When you've seen nothing but water for weeks on end, a Louis L'Amour novel describing a slow-running brook lined with cottonwood trees, a ranch house, and cattle grazing in green pastures, paints a welcome picture in one's mind.

I happen to believe the answer to any question or the solution to any problem is written somewhere on the pages of a book. There are two problems that if eliminated would no doubt solve the problems of the world, and those two things are hunger and illiteracy.

Whether it be my stories you read or others, please continue to read books and the world will become a much better place.

Acknowledgements

I must first say thank you to those who read my first book, *An Angel is Born*. I'll never forget the honor I felt when the first person read that book and I feel that same honor with each new reader. However, there is a lot that goes into the making of a book and a writer must have a team of supporters in order to succeed. Any writer who does it all on his own is either a liar or a much better man than I.

A writer must have a good editor and there are none better than Angela Weichman. Thank you, Angie, for your editing genius and your special touch. I would also like to thank Judith Palmateer of Amber Skye publishing for your motivational help, advice and mentoring. Thanks to my sweetheart and personal adviser Jessica Stockwell. Thanks to my niece, Savanna, for her artistic skills in illustration.

I would also like to thank my new friend, Beth Fuhrmann, who was kind enough to read *An Angel is*

Born as well as my new manuscript. Beth is a natural born proof reader and editor all in one.

Last but certainly not least I wish to express my genuine appreciation for the help and advice of Jamie Fischer. I've never been able to figure her out as a person; I'll leave Jamie to her mysteries. But I will have to say that without her help and motivation this book would not have been written.

66481550R00145

Made in the USA
Lexington, KY
15 August 2017